Love/Imperfect

T0040391

Also by **Christopher T. Leland**

FICTION

Mean Time
Mrs. Randall
The Book of Marvels
The Professor of Aesthetics
Letting Loose

NON-FICTION

The Last Happy Men: The Generation of 1922,
  Fiction, and the Argentine Reality
The Art of Compelling Fiction
The Creative Writer's Style Guide

Love/Imperfect

STORIES BY

Christopher T. Leland

Wayne State University Press Detroit

15 14 13 12 11   5 4 3 2 1

Library of Congress Cataloging-in-Publication Data

Leland, Christopher T.
Love/imperfect / Christopher T. Leland.
p. cm. — Made in Michigan writers series
ISBN 978-0-8143-3495-9 (pbk. : alk. paper)
I. Title.
PS3562.E4637L68 2011
813'.54—dc22
2010042159

∞

Designed and typeset by Maya Rhodes
Composed in Adobe Caslon and Meta

The following stories have appeared elsewhere in slightly different form:

"Fellatio," *Dogwood Review*, 2006.
"Memento Mori," *Harrington Gay Men's Fiction Quarterly*, vol. 7, no. 4, 2006.
"As If in Time of War," *River Walk*, 2006.
"Reprise," *Cardinalis: A Journal of Ideas*, Summer 2003.

For my nephews:
Benjamin, Daniel, Julian, and Marshall.

For my niece,
Eraine.

For my namesake,
Sylvia.

Contents

Love/Imperfect

In Conclusion

for Jo

He would always wonder if she knew anybody unextraordinary.

He could see her from the breakfast nook. In her housecoat, her hair pinned loosely back from her face, she looked like a *Hausfrau* in a German movie. But she was smoking—smoking "elegantly," he thought. It was not an accusation. She was not conscious of how she smoked. But she held the cigarette in a way that showed study—a one-time calculation now become reflex, like the movements of a skilled toe dancer.

He could hear Leon playing next-door.

"What's that?" he had asked that first morning.

"Leon." She looked up from the paper with her light, slightly indulgent grin.

"Who's Leon?"

"The man next-door."

She went back to reading, but he could see the smile widen in her eyes.

"Should we call the Humane Society?"

She laughed then, a smooth breath gliding effortlessly into: "You're terrible, Freddy. You are!" She touched his hand. "Leon could have played professionally, you know. That's what Alec told me. Some orchestra back East offered him a chair. Years ago. He didn't take it though. Or couldn' t . . ." Her fingers rustled the hair on his arm. "He should have. He loves the clarinet. He plays it when he's sad. . . ."

"Oh, he's sad all right," he said as he kissed her.

She pushed him gently away. "Don't make fun of Leon. Leon's really an extraordinary man."

She brought breakfast on a tray. They could have set the toaster on the table, scooped jam from a jar, fought the wax paper off a stick of margarine. But the tray, with the carafe and stoneware cups, the plate of toast, and little saucers of jelly and butter shavings, gave breakfast a perfection he had at first found disquieting.

But for her, it was right: graceful as her walk, free from the danger of accidents. If the toast burned, it smoked off-stage. The burble of the coffee maker did not drown out the birdsong from outdoors.

"So you have to go today?"

"Yes." It was a lie as transparent as the next. "I'll be back down soon though. It shouldn't be long."

She nodded. "That's what Alec and I said, you know, when we couldn't stand it any longer. We said only for a little while, so he could paint. . . ."

o o o

"He was a painter. Is a painter, I suppose I should say." She gestured behind her with her cigarette, a languid movement of her arm like a strand of kelp in the sea. Her bracelets jangled. "Everything on that wall is his. His style's changed since. He's much less abstract." She shook her head and looked up at him with soulful and bemusing solemnity. "He used to be an extraordinary painter."

At the party, when they were introduced, she had asked him: "Do you paint?"

It was hard to hear above the music and the other conversations. Though he was tired from hitchhiking, her attention flattered him. He eyed her appreciatively, aiming for the right reply.

"Houses sometimes. I painted curbs for the county once."

She laughed, and he felt a shudder in the small of his back.

"We could talk better on the deck."

"What's a nine-letter word for 'ineffectiveness'?" The pencil poised over the paper crumpled on her knee, her mouth full of toast, she should not have looked so refined. Too refined to be innocent.

"I don't know." He put his elbows heavily on the table.

She did not look up. "Harold . . . I've talked about him, remember? He was the professor I knew after Alec left. Harold did the crossword every morning. He always had to finish before he could eat his breakfast."

"Must've liked brunch," he said sourly, sipping coffee.

"Not at all. He had a gift for them. He was . . ."—she brought her head up slowly, till he could feel her eyes on him, cool as gunmetal— ". . . really quite . . ."

". . . a nice place. Alec did well when we were married. At first, it was awful—no money, there in the Bay Area. That's where we met." She took his arm and led him down into the living room, all chrome and corners and primary colors. "Where you're from, isn't it? Oakland or something? You're Tom's little brother's roommate?" She smiled, self-satisfied, as she ferried him toward the sofa. "Poor Alec. If only he hadn't been so unprepossessing, if you know what I mean." She half-reclined on the cushions and beckoned him beside her. She rested her head on his thigh. "I'm simply exhausted. Mandy's parties are always so frenetic!" She bit off the word in displeasure, then sighed. "Alec was so earnest. Earnestness can be unbearable, you know."

He stroked her hair, blond from the pool and tennis.

She turned her head suddenly and nipped his finger. "I hope you're horribly insincere."

"Couldn't you rent a car or something?"

He snorted a laugh. "Right. And go down on the agent to pay for it?"

"Don't say things like that." It was only half-jesting. "It's too early in the day to say things like that."

He heard her voice, soft like the darkness. "Do you say things when you make love?"

His fingers toyed with the straps of her dress. "What kind of things?"

"Oh, you know. Extraordinary things." She shivered slightly, almost giggled as he passed his hands around her waist. "Vulgar things."

He pushed the straps from her shoulders. Her gown fell off her in a whisper. Against the hair of his chest, her breasts made a fine, dry sound like a kiss.

"I'll say any fucking thing you want."

"Did you want me when you first saw me?" The glow of her cigarette lit her face each time she inhaled, reflecting in her half-closed eyes. "I wanted you, you know."

"Oh?" He curled beside her, sated, smiling, waiting for her warmth against him so they could fall asleep.

"Yes. From the moment I saw you. I knew almost everybody else. You looked a little shabby, by the way. You should get a new jacket."

"Uh-huh." The mattress was deep and thick and different from the ones in rented rooms.

"I didn't know how to approach you." She snuffed out the cigarette. "So young. Fresh-faced. I almost decided you were queer. You aren't, are you?"

He turned on his side, propping his head in one hand and running the other up to her shoulder. "What do you think?"

"I guess not." She kissed him. "But then, you can never really tell. There's always something funny about the men I care for. . . ."

o o o

She gathered the dishes, silent. He went to the bedroom and finished packing what little he had in his duffel bag. It was heavier than it had been two weeks before. He glanced around the room one last time, trying to submerge the night before in details, in the various treasures he had come to know from extraordinary Paris and extraordinary Rome. . . .

She was as nice about it as a woman can ever be.

. . . extraordinary Lima and extraordinary Seoul . . .

Maybe there had been just one too many.

. . . extraordinary Peter and extraordinary Saul . . .

Maybe they had all been just a bit too extraordinary.

He tossed the bag over his shoulder and walked clumsily out of the bedroom. The sack had become an uncomfortable thing. She was waiting for him at the front door with a sandwich wrapped in plastic and an orange.

She looked somehow preposterous.

"You're not wearing your new jacket!"

"I don't want it to get dirty on the road."

She nodded, glanced away. "Don't be long, Freddy." She bussed him on the cheek.

"No."

Outside, the morning was still gold and misty. There would be plenty of traffic. At the head of the walk, he looked back and saw her on the porch, a cigarette burning blue in her hand, her posture casual and perfect as a marble goddess.

He wondered if, by next week, he would be extraordinary.

He could hear Leon playing next-door.

The Woman Who Loved Claude Rains

That I.J. and Ina Bannister were one of the couples in Rhymers Creek who made least sense was pretty much agreed on. That, from time to time and as years go by, a man and the woman he takes to wife live lives distinctive and sometimes at odds isn't really something that calls much attention. But I.J. and Ina's marriage was one of two people so completely divergent that they might have been not merely from different backgrounds, but different planets. Nobody ever quite figured out why it lasted, though lasted it had.

From what I knew, which was a fair amount really, because back then Rhymers Creek was still a pretty small place and everybody probably knew just a bit too much about everybody else's business, there was a real stew when she decided to marry I.J. He was ten years older than she was, and known far and wide as a man's man who had long said that he really couldn't see that he had much use for a wife. And Ina, if she wasn't the prettiest girl around was certainly the most viva-

cious, seemed about the last person in the world appropriate for somebody as surly as I.J. There were endless explanations for it: Ina was just
looking for another father, not a husband; Ina had been out at Skeeter
Henderson's roadhouse one night, left with I.J., gotten pregnant, and
so married him; Ina had been out at Skeeter Henderson's roadhouse
one night, left with someone else, gotten pregnant, and I.J. had married her as a favor to her family, and so on and so forth.

All of these seemed equally reasonable and nonsensical.

So, unsatisfying as it was, Rhymers Creek was left with the oldest
explanation of all: that love obeys no rules of justice or logic, of like
attracting like, but, of its own volition, is silly and whimsical, so those
struck by Cupid's arrows are fully capable of making choices—real and
honest choices—that defy all predictions and explanations of the rest
of humankind.

It was the summer my cousin Donnie got me the job at I.J. Bannister's
Garage and Esso, telling my dad it was about time I started to earn
a little money. When we were alone, of course, he told me that, at
sixteen, I ought to be able to pick up a little nooky from some of the
girls who passed through on Friday and Saturday nights, when I.J. left
the station in Donnie's hands. I really didn't believe most of the stories Donnie told me about making out with half the girls in Rhymers
Creek back by the trashcans, and, even though he swore up and down
it was true, I was sure the story about some woman named Lydia passing through on her way to Marysville (whom, Donnie said, he had
screwed in the ladies room) was bullshit.

My theory was that Donnie was just looking for a way to justify the
fact that he'd been working at I.J.'s long enough to make it obvious that
that was the place he was going to work for the rest of his life. He'd
started years before, when Dewey Monroe got put away for murder,

and he'd been there ever since. He was close to thirty, so old that I, at sixteen, looked upon him as I might have looked upon my own father—someone of a generation so distant that he might well not really know what screwing was.

It might not have been so bad, except that everybody said out loud that, when I.J. passed, the whole business would go lock, stock, and barrel, to his son, Lloyd, whom everybody called Junior, and he had always hated the garage and worked for the county and told anybody who'd listen that he'd up and sell the whole shebang when he got his hands on it. In my family, about all we could hope is that I.J. lasted a good long time, because otherwise nobody really knew what Donnie would do without I.J. and the station—or what we would do with Donnie.

But the truth was, I didn't mind getting on at the gas station. It would turn out I'd live my adult life in the three cities in America where you didn't need to own a car, but nobody could have told me that at the time. In those days, all the whole country ever thought about was cars, especially those who'd just gotten their driver's licenses, and it didn't seem like a bad idea at all to learn something about transmissions and carburetors and brake shoes. I thought the shirt I had to wear, blue with its little oval patch that said "Mel," looked goofy, but nobody really kidded me about it, and, before my first week was out, I'd really settled in pretty well at I.J.'s.

That wasn't much thanks to I.J. It was mostly Donnie who took care of whatever training was involved in pumping gas and checking the oil and that sort of thing. About all I got from I.J. was a boot in the butt a couple times when he thought I was screwing around. That didn't surprise me much, since everybody knew I.J. Bannister was never the easiest man to get along with in this world. If his business had depended on his personality, I doubt the Esso people would have been too pleased that he held their franchise in Rhymers Creek. I.J. wasn't mean, really, just gruff and quick to get mad and not very patient with people who tried to tell him how to do his job, which, where cars were concerned, meant just about everybody. The way he saw it, people didn't second-guess their doctors or their dentists or Harley at the appliance store who told them that Amanas were a good buy right now, so why should they feel they had the right to stick their noses over his shoulder when he was halfway into an engine to ask, "Well, what about the timing?" or say how it couldn't be the rods and maybe it was just the plugs that needed changing? He didn't appreciate that kind of interference at all, and he wasn't shy about telling anybody so.

He probably did lose some business that way, but he said at least he kept his pride, and when it came down to it, he was such a crackerjack mechanic that most everybody swallowed his resentment and left it to I.J. to tell him what his Dodge or Chevy was ailing from.

The other reason people suffered I.J., I suspect, was Ina, who, as I've said, was about as different from her husband as it was possible to be. If there were times when he reminded you of a man turned into somebody's cranky grampa long before his time, she seemed more like a perpetual debutante, which ought to have made her seem silly, but, instead, endeared her to just about everyone. Ever since Junior went to junior high school, she had worked at The Palace of Fashion, and there wasn't a woman in town who didn't swear by her taste in dresses and shoes and the right accessories. And with men, she had a peculiar flirtatiousness that made them feel appreciated without ever confusing her attentions with a real attempt at seduction, or so I believed at the time.

Ina herself drove a 1956 Chrysler Imperial. It had fold-down armrests in front and back, ashtrays right, left, and center for every possible passenger, and was painted cream up top and turquoise on the bottom because the late 'fifties was the age of two-tone: maroon and cream, cobalt and white, like the banners of the colleges nine-tenths of the boys who admired those cars would never attend.

The first time I had seen her at the station, she floated out of the July heat like the diaphanous fairy of some children's book, in white dress and white hat and white gloves, about as different from I.J. Bannister—eternally covered with a patina of grease and oil—as anyone could be. She stood there shimmering in the waves of mirage that rose off the asphalt, and they actually kissed with what I would, years later, know as an "air-kiss," but nobody then in Rhymers Creek would even think to call it that in those days.

And that very first time, I realized he somehow adored her—he rough and dirty and nasty in the way he talked and moved and acted—thrilling and at the same time ugly for a high school boy he kicked in the butt when he felt like it.

And she? She needing rescue, a damsel, some slightly faded dream of femininity: a bit buxom but not too, not a Marilyn or Ava, but rather a Bergman. Not as flat as Audrey Hepburn, but perhaps that sultry new star, Kim Novak, we all felt obligated to adore.

I.J. kissed her, and she him, his hands not reaching for her body, all that gorgeous whiteness, nor she for that dark, slick male stockiness. I.J. was built like a bear. A short, square bear, I'll admit, but a bear nonetheless. I could not understand it then, those grownups, me sixteen and awonder they would even find themselves in the same orbit, the same universe. But I knew very little then, and the Bannisters, quite unexpectedly, ultimately taught me quite a lot.

You must remember what we were like then. We were the sons of murderers, and it was as if, in grief and horror at what they had done, they had to make for us an innocent world they themselves had never known—children of the Roaring 'Twenties and Groaning 'Thirties.

So we matured in that false purity that followed the war—the one the next decade would blow to kingdom come—with a kind of astonishing foolishness neither those who came before nor those who came after could ever quite believe.

The first time I truly met Ina, was actually introduced to Ina, when she knew me by my name as opposed to someone glimpsed as "Mel" (Mel had been killed out on Blood Alley, on the highway towards Marysville, barely three hundred yards from where Bobby Demmers had been killed years before, in exactly the same kind of head-on) was after I had been at the station almost a month. I had seen the Chrysler and the air-kissing and so on a dozen times, but this particular day, she swept in, always grand in that car, immaculate and somewhere just past her prime, and she honked the horn and gestured me over.

I went to her, parked at pump 4, in my hat and my hardcloth uniform. "Hello, Mrs. Bannister," I said with the practiced heartiness that I.J. demanded.

She had unrolled her window, and she smiled winningly. For me at sixteen, she was not that much younger than I.J., but still she did seem younger. Was it happier or just a little mad?

"Mel?" she said, looking at my nametag, and then she said, "You can't be Mel. Mel's dead. You must be that nice boy I.J. told me about. You're Donnie's cousin." She paused. "Barker, isn't it? You're Barker MacKay."

"Yes, ma'am," I said.

The MacKays, you must understand, had never really meant anything in Rhymers Creek, in Mockdon County, or much of anywhere else. Mine was poor Scotch-Irish stock that was common as dirt up and down the East Coast and never had any pretensions. My own family had vaguely come from Pennsylvania sometime, drifting west and then south and then southwest, each place promising to be a little more inviting than the last, and then cousins and nephews and probably (though this was never spoken of) bastard kin would follow and we would have to find a new nest to flee to until, in later years, the Pacific finally stopped us.

"I.J.," she said meaningfully, suddenly opening the door. "I.J. has spoken highly of you."

She smoothed her white dress. That day she was wearing sunglasses with ridiculous wings, exactly what children thirty or forty years later would affect when they wanted to evoke those times. They had rhinestones set around the borders.

"Is he here?"

"No, ma'am," I said quickly, deferentially. "He had to go with Donnie to get some transmissions in Marysville. They left early, when I first got here. It's me and Timmy and Boz that's minding the store."

Boz was the dog, a mutt with a limp that I.J. kept alive God knew how. Timmy was my second or third cousin (we were never sure) and he spent most of his time—at least, when I.J. was away and couldn't kick *his* butt—trying to make time with his eternally faithless girlfriend, Marjorie, who had been married once and kept an apartment on the Square that everybody said was paid for by the lawyer Sammy Stephens, who had the apartment down the hall.

"I see," she said frostily.

It sounded strange to me, that chill, since I had never questioned why we would need some transmissions here and there at I.J.'s Garage and Esso, if garage and Esso we were to be.

Then Ina looked at me strangely. "Take my car to the side, will you, Barker?" And she then swept into the office there at the station. She had left her keys in the ignition—something people did commonly then, filled with trust and perhaps too a sense that anybody would immediately recognize anybody else's car, and so call the state police if it had been stolen.

I did as I was told. I was sixteen then, after all, and to be sixteen then was not to be sixteen ten or twenty years later, or, for that matter, sixteen a decade or more before. It was a strange time out of time, and we were much younger then than our fathers or sons would be.

It was slow at the station. It was a Thursday morning in August, unforgivingly hot in Rhymers Creek, the wet of a storm that threatened but would not come hanging over the town like a soggy blanket. I came into the office, with its windows open and three fans trying to do the work that would later be that of an air conditioner, and Ina was there, slowly whipping a mimeographed flyer about a special on W-30 oil through the air, sitting on the Naugahyde sofa I.J. had placed next to a display of Delco spark plugs.

She looked up when I came in. Me, sixteen. She looked at me not hard but in serious appraisal. I don't think anybody, except perhaps I.J. when he hired me, had looked at me quite in that way before.

"Barker," she said, and it had a fine, almost aristocratic sound out of her mouth atop all that white. "Barker, could you buy me a Coke?"

I stopped momentarily and then started to dig in my pocket. "Yes, ma'am. Just a . . ."

"No, no," she smiled. "There's change in my purse."

"No, I'll . . . I'll get it from the register."

I was mesmerized by her, that diaphanous, tightly busted body. She had a sweet face with the reddest lipstick I had ever seen splicing across it, the kind that would stain a cigarette butt with the deepest mark of woman.

"No!" It was abrupt and not to be questioned. She smiled wider, handing me the nickel. "No. I.J. will think you shorted him. Take this."

She was right, of course. I.J. would say we were a nickel short, and Donnie and Timmy and me would have to come up with what was missing. Somewhere—and later I would suspect I knew why—he had learned not to trust other people, but that would be later.

I took Ina's nickel. "Get one for you, too," she said, and she extracted a second coin from her purse.

"Yes, ma'am," I said stupidly.

I went outside and brought back the two six-ounce Cokes, the bottles bleeding already in the heat.

She took an almost swaggering sip—not demure, a full, deep swig that should have made her belch. But she was as assuredly someone who did not belch as Jesus did not fart. She made a soft, pleased sound after she took the bottle from her lips, looked at me as if she herself might have represented "The Pause That Refreshes," and said: "Do you know, Barker, that you remind me of Claude Rains?"

I had, that summer, as a sign of my growing maturity—as a sign that if, as Cousin Donnie had suggested, it was time I earned some money and, perhaps, get myself a little nooky—affected the accoutrements of a man of the world and grown a mustache. It was relatively paltry then—not the worst mustache, but not exactly what Errol Flynn sported, nor certainly that precise, clipped, sophisticated hair-on-lip that I knew from late-show presentations of *Casablanca.*

I snorted some Coke through my nose when she said it, which burned incredibly. For I, at sixteen, could hardly imagine I might look, especially in a uniform with "Mel" on the breast, like Louis Renault or the much wickeder and unmustached man Claude Rains played in *Notorious.*

There was a very strange pause.

Ina looked at me then with something like pity. Perhaps something like contempt. Yet, too, it was a prideful look.

"There was a time, Barker, when Isaac looked like Claude Rains."

I don't know that I had ever heard anyone refer to I.J. by his Christian name. I don't know that then I even knew it.

"I'm sorry, ma'am, I didn't mean to . . ."

She turned her head then, beneficent. "No, Barker, don't apologize." She took another sip of her Coke, more demure now. "I was a woman who always loved Claude Rains, even back to his first movies. I adored *Invisible Man,* almost everything he did in the '30s, really. He reminds me," she said with a conscious wistfulness, "of when I was young."

There was a long moment then. I was not smart enough, I will admit, to understand what she probably intended—that Claude and I.J. and I all resembling one another was an invitation for me to play a part I would likely have regretted for infinite reasons.

And she might have regretted as well.

I stared at her stupidly—or so I imagine now—and Ina looked at me.

And then she sighed.

"Tell I.J. I was here," she said simply, setting the half-emptied bottle on the floor. "Tell him I'll wait for him for supper."

"Yes, ma'am," I repeated and swept her Coke up and drained mine.

As she got into her Chrysler, she reached out suddenly and squeezed my hand. "Don't you cut that mustache," she said.

And I said, "Oh, ma'am, when I go back to school, the coach'll make me."

"You boys." She shook her head sadly. "You boys with each other." She sighed again. "Well, we'll just make believe, and when there's no coach to make you, you keep it. You understand me?"

I stood there dumbly. I realized then I had been propositioned a few minutes before by an older woman, just what Donnie had told me about.

Hadn't I?

And I should have responded, but the moment was lost now, and I was not sure I would have wanted to anyway.

"Yes, ma'am," I said as I shut her door. "I will grow it back just as soon as I can, I promise."

She motored away then—not drove, motored like the English say. I stood breathless beside the pumps, stood there till a car pulled in for a fill-up and oil check ten minutes later.

I never saw Ina Bannister alone again, and it was only later that I understood why she had made the quiet proposition she had over bottles of Coca-Cola on a blistering August afternoon.

One night, two summers later, as I packed my bags for Amherst, an institution that had given me a great deal of money to come there, I wandered by I.J.'s very late at night and, in the dim shadows of the garage through the new, glass-paneled doors, saw Donnie and I.J. going down on each other. I was drunk (times were already beginning to turn), but I said nothing to anyone and wondered if I might have gone down on I.J. or he on me when I was sixteen and so turned him into that mysterious Lydia who had passed through and Donnie took in the bathroom.

But in that moment, I thought of Ina, and I thought of I.J. too, and the world that was Rhymers Creek and that remains Rhymers Creek in so many places, and even then, in that long ago time in that, for me, long ago place, I admired them for having found one another, for having loved one another, for having made their peace with one other.

The moment I arrived at Amherst, I grew a mustache, and that mustache I have kept through all these years.

Donnie stayed at the station till I.J. was dead, till Junior closed it and sold the property, and on that site they built a new hotel.

For the rest, I can only hope that sometime, somewhere, Ina found some other man or boy who reminded her of Claude Rains.

Though maybe not.

Maybe that was never the point at all.

He came to get her at two o'clock, when the smog had begun to back up in the canyons and settle across the valley. It was hot for March. He did not get out of the car, honking instead since the appointment was at three. She hopped down the walk in her new sundress, the first time she had worn it since he bought it for her two Sundays ago at Penney's. She had curled her hair. When she got in the car, he could smell the perfume she usually used only in the evening.

"I was afraid you couldn't get away," she said as she kissed him.

He started down the street toward the freeway on-ramp. "Naw. No problem. Bill was cool. Lotsa traffic though." He glanced at her. "You sure got duded up."

"Well," she flipped down the visor to check her makeup in the mirror, "we should make a good impression."

"What the hell!" he snorted. "It's them who want to take our money, not the other way around."

"Larry. It's not that." She frowned. "It's just . . . things are going to be different. We're going to have to be a little more, I don't know, dressy."

He shook his head and pulled onto 57. She slid across the seat to be closer to him and slipped her arm through his like she always did. The diamond caught the sunlight, and he peeked down to see it bobbing as she tapped time to the song on the radio. Linda had said it was "garish" and too expensive when they went to Zales with Luis and Al.

Mo-ther, she had said when they got home. *Look at it. Just look at it. Glass, that's what it looks like. Kathy'll think it's just glass.*

Linda had never liked Kathy. She never made any secret of it. When she was home from school in San Luis, Linda would always find a way to bring it up. *Are you still seeing Kathy?* she'd say, or *Kathy's nice, but the two of you together, Larry. She looks funny next to you, you know what I mean?* And when he told her to lay off, she would start on the job and why wasn't he in school: *A grease monkey. You want to be a grease monkey all your life? You could at least take something at the JC, just to keep your mind alive.*

"Give me a cigarette, honey."

He didn't like her smoking. It looked tough. Linda always told him Kathy looked tough. *She looks like she oughta be on the back of a motorcycle,* she'd say. He'd tell her to go fuck herself, except when their mother was around. Then he'd just tell her she was jealous. *Jealous, ha!* And Mom would say, *Don't ding at him, Linda,* and that would end it.

He felt her hand in his pocket. "Do you want one?" she asked.

"Yeah. Yeah, sure." He liked her fingers there and smiled a little.

She was scared. It was like this was a job interview or something, like they'd call her in a week to let her know how she'd done.

She lit both cigarettes and slipped one between his lips.

He actually had thought she was a little tough when he met her. She was a friend of Al's sister, and she spent most of the afternoon at Puddingstone on the hood of the Camaro, watching them water ski and drinking CC hidden in a paper bag. He hardly talked to her till the rental on the boat was almost up. Her bathing suit was so tight, he was afraid he was showing it. They really didn't get too much said, because she was pretty drunk by then, but, after they shared a joint, they did make out for a while late in the day. She smelled of whiskey and weed and got so anxious it made him a little scared.

They went out together with Al and Doris for a while, and then it was just them. He was a little surprised she was still a virgin. He took her cherry after seven weeks.

That, he remembered, was three years ago last November. It was cold in that park at two in the morning, and neither of them cared at all.

Kathy pulled at his wrist every so often to look at the time. It made him nervous. After they got through Santa Ana, he pushed the Dodge up to seventy-five.

"Watch out for cops," he said.

"Do you think we'll be late?"

"Don't sweat it!" He sighed. "He's not gonna run off if we're not there right on time."

When he told them at the shop that he and Kathy were going to move to MiraMission after the wedding, Al whistled: *Shee-it! You put one ball down on that ring. You gonna let them take the other one for the down?* Luis looked hurt and shook his head: *That's a long way, man.* And Bill, who worried about hours since he was the owner, bitched about how Larry would be later than ever every morning. They razzed him the rest of the day about it, about how pretty soon he'd move to Newport Beach and have his nose stuck so far up in the air he'd be sniffing angel ass.

Finally, he got mad and threw down his wrench. "Shit, who wants to stay in fuckin' Pomona the rest of his life!"

They all looked ashamed. Al said, "It's cool, man. We're just shittin' around."

They laughed it off and got drunk together after work to celebrate, but Larry didn't get into it like he thought he should.

On the way home, after he let Luis off, he felt really strange, like he was going to cry or something.

MiraMission was all new: jet-black streets winding past sparkling white condos, row on row, each one with a Bermuda grass lawn smooth as a pool table and a pathetic cuestick of a tree staked out in front. A couple dwarf pines flanked each rust-red front door, and every jamb had five black numbers at eye level on the right side: 20561, 20563, 20565.

The streets were all named for former boxing champions: Robinson Way and Firpo Drive and Patterson Court.

"It's so beautiful, isn't it, honey?" Kathy sighed.

"Uh-huh."

He had hoped there would be people out mowing their lawns or sitting on the curb, watching toddlers in the sprinklers or playing catch, just so he could get a feel for the place. But there was no one: no Toros sputtering, no kids, nobody with the car jacked up. He didn't see a single basketball hoop.

But it was Tuesday, after all. Couldn't expect people to be out like it was Sunday afternoon.

They stopped in front of 19293 Johannnsen Circle, a cul-de-sac off Jack Dempsey Drive. On the porch, the realtor came out to greet them, a thirtyish man with horn-rim glasses and a paunch. Kathy didn't move.

Larry got out, stood for a moment, then walked around and opened her door.

She didn't thank him. It was as if he always did it.

"You must be the couple-to-be. Congratulations!" The realtor came down the walk, his hand extended. "Tom Bellinger."

"Larry Edmundson." The handshake was firm, careful, not too long and not too short. It reminded Larry of his teachers at high school graduation. "This is Kathy."

"It's a real pleasure, Kathy." Tom was all teeth. Teeth and glasses and a good, fat stomach. "Come on up." He motioned them toward the front door with a broad sweep of his arm. "Let me show you the place."

All the walls inside were white. The drapes were white. The carpet was a beigey-gray or grayish-beige. It was hard to describe exactly.

"We're very proud of MiraMission Glen," Tom was saying. "It's one of the best planned developments in the area, you know. The Realtor's Association gave it a special citation for design. It was in the *Times* a couple weeks back."

Larry couldn't tell exactly where the living room stopped and the dining room started. Different from his father's house, but that was a place nearly fifty years old—a bungalow from the 'twenties his folks picked up for cheap right after the Korean War. Even then, as he remembered, the trees around it were thick and broad-limbed, and out back there was an orange grove.

"We're very proud of what we've accomplished here." They were on the patio, brick-paved, with a high wooden fence around it—eight feet or more—to separate it from the carport. "By next year, the shopping center down on ValleyVista Boulevard will be done. You can do all your grocery shopping there, and there'll be a drugstore and some boutiques, of course. And the regional mall's only a hop, skip, and jump up MiraMission Road. Will you be working around here, Larry?"

The question caught him off-guard. He'd never really thought about leaving the job in Pomona.

"Naw. I mean, I'm happy . . ."

"Larry's with an automotive firm," Kathy said steadily, precisely. "He'll be able to get on with one down here in a month or two."

He smiled. A "firm." Bill would shit a brick if he heard somebody call the shop a firm.

They were in the kitchen. "Completely equipped," Tom Bellinger was saying. "All electric." All white: white tiles, white stove, white Frigidaire. "The disposal comes with all of our homes . . . only the latest. . . . The ice-maker/water dispenser is one of our most popular features."

At home, in summer, all summers, there was an old glass milk bottle in the refrigerator. Year after year, the same bottle Larry was always forgetting to refill: Linda whining about it, Mom scolding vaguely, Dad unconcerned at all except for at least once each August when he really wanted that cold drink and there was no beer and the water bottle was empty and *Goddamn it, boy! I'm takin my belt off! Why the hell can't . . .*

Upstairs, the carpet was ocean blue. One whole wall of the master bedroom was a closet with mirrored doors. Larry smiled. They could put the bed opposite it—a king-size, maybe even a water bed—and it would be like one of those Triple-X motels in Hollywood.

"Nice layout."

"Most everybody's pleased with it," Tom said—was it that blandly?—motioning them to the balcony.

Kathy sighed.

"There's no smog here in MiraMission." He was proud of that. It was in his voice. "Every evening, after the work's done, you can sit out here and enjoy the sun. A west facing's in demand. We ask a little more for it, but it's worth it, don't you think?"

They looked over the carports to the ravine behind, out across the valley, past the other condos and the Shell station and the freeway and the McDonald's at the next off-ramp, on toward the sea twelve miles away.

"It's just divine," Kathy whispered. She never said "divine." It was a fag word she would have made fun of. "How are the schools here?"

Tom smiled knowingly. "Well, of course, things are just getting off the ground. But by the time you two need to worry about it, we'll be all established. The high school opens in the fall and the JC's on the drawing boards right now. And, of course, the university's only fifteen minutes by freeway."

Larry shifted, uncomfortable.

"Oh, Larry, we could take some courses."

"Yeah, keep our minds alive."

They started back downstairs.

"This is a wonderful place for a family just starting out. It's an easy drive to the city, but there aren't the problems. No gangs. No drugs."

Larry smirked at Kathy, who ignored him.

"And there's the recreation area. It's like living on a cruise ship! It keeps the neighborhood so quiet. No kids ripping and racing. They're so busy, they don't have time to get into mischief. Come on, we'll walk over."

Mischief. Larry almost said it aloud. No mischief! It was a word he had always hated, a word nobody but a grandmother could get away with. *Trouble.* That's what he got into, or didn't. *Don't get into any trouble,* his mother would say. In Pomona, there were a thousand ways to get in trouble, depending on how old you were: stealing oranges or pinching candy and pens or even a carton of cigarettes at the Thrifty; scoring some beers or some grass; getting crosswise with the lowriders or the gangs from Sin City.

Or the cops.

And then, of course, there was getting a girl in trouble.

Here, maybe there was just mischief.

The park had a black iron fence around it. Tom unlocked the gate to let them in, then reached into his pocket and took out two gummed labels. They had happy faces on them and said: "Hi! My name is _____, your new neighbor." He filled in "Larry" and "Kathy."

They looked around. It was pretty. Everything was organized. Leagues and teams and Rams and Raiders. There was a great pool, and there were scores on the wall of the fastest swimmers.

The basketball courts were empty.

"Nobody plays much until fall," Tom explained. "That's when the season gets started."

"Don't seem real popular anyhow. Didn't see any hoops in the driveways."

Tom shook his head. "Oh, the Homeowners Association won't allow that. You let people put something like that up and, before you know it, you've ruined the neighborhood. We have rules about planting and draperies, almost anything that would change the appearance of the unit.

"Besides, the kids would make lots of noise. Here in MiraMission Glen, things are laid out so there are places for playing and places for quiet, gracious living."

That's what the brochures said, the ones Tom gave them when they were back inside: *Quiet, gracious living . . . MiraMission Glen, a community planned with all your needs in mind . . . a world apart . . . free from the hustle and bustle, but still in the heart of growing MiraMission, a prestige community . . . Serene and secure . . .*

For the last half hour, Kathy had said hardly anything at all. She had taken it all in—the house and the recreation area and the brochures, with the look Larry remembered from when he gave her the ring, a look of pleasure born of disbelief. He watched her curiously out of the corner of his eye as Tom Bellinger talked about financing.

"Now, for a young couple just starting out . . . A big investment . . . But in today's financial climate . . . Real estate prices aren't going anywhere but up."

It was everything Pomona wasn't, everything she had dreamed about, he could tell. *Gracious. Serene. Prestige. A good place to raise kids.* Kids. A swimming pool and tennis courts and the university just fifteen minutes by freeway to keep your mind alive.

"Easy terms! Couples just like you . . . Apartment living just doesn't make sense."

No gangs. No drugs. No boys in the street. No basketball hoops or neighbors who don't mow their yards. No people of different colors—just white, white, white as the walls and the drapes and the Frigidaire.

"Now, let me give you my card."

They were by the car. Kathy was standing a little apart, gazing up the street, a breeze rippling her new sundress and freshly curled hair.

Larry could smell just the shadow of that perfume.

They would move here.

It was what she wanted.

And, at that moment, he wanted to give her what she wanted more than anything else in the world.

"We'll give you a call," he was saying. He was speaking mechanically to toothy, four-eyed Tom Bellinger. "I need to talk to my folks. And Kathy's. And the bank."

"Of course. Of course! Buying a home is a big decision. But you'll decide it's the right one, for sure."

They shook hands again, and Kathy turned and smiled. Larry opened her door, then got in the Dodge. As they drove away, she looked back to watch Tom waving good-bye.

When they got to the freeway, she said, "Let's drive to the beach, honey."

The sun was in their eyes as they headed toward San Clemente. They did not talk.

Finally, Larry said, "Well?"

"We could afford it," she said determinedly. "We can! Even if I have to get two jobs."

"The commute'll be a bitch, and that's gonna cost, too."

"But you don't have to stay at Bill's. There hafta be some places down here. And they probably pay better."

He felt a lump in his stomach.

On the beach, it was chilly. He put his arm around her, and they kissed. He wanted to do her right there in the sand, but there were too many people.

And her dress was new.

"Let's eat," he said with an urgency just this side of panic. "Let's eat in Newport."

It cost a lot. They had cocktails and lobster and a bottle of wine. It would mean no slice of pie with the girls after work for Kathy, no trip to the bar with Luis and Al and Bill for him. But that wasn't much of a price, Larry thought, for the way Kathy looked and the way she talked and the way she said: "Oh, honey, it'll be just perfect."

And Pomona sure wasn't perfect.

Perfect you have to pay for. You give things up for—water bottles and garage backboards and Luis and Al, so things can be as perfect as those basketball courts and the pool table lawns and those white, white walls.

When dinner was done, when the wine was through and they were both a little tipsy, they walked through Newport, past the restaurants and sportswear shops and the houses that faced the water—all clean and quiet and rich.

They came to the beach. Larry held Kathy close. Together, they stared into the blackness of the sea at night.

And behind them, glittering, shimmering not in moonlight but in one they made all by themselves, rose the freeways and movie shows, the shopping centers and office plazas, the service stations and Golden Arches . . .

The temples and palaces of the New Jerusalem.

The Congregation of Love

for Forrest

If it hadn't been for that goddamn magazine, Billy Paul would still be alive today.

I don't know why he even talked to them, except that a man in the condition he was in can hardly think his way to the bathroom straight, much less do anything else. That reporter just showed up on his doorstep, and he said she was so nice and pretty and everything that he wanted to help her out, so he signed the form she gave him and talked to her and showed her the pictures and even some of the letters. Then she took off, and, three weeks later, all of Mockdon County is whooping it up in every drugstore and supermarket about how old Billy Paul's made *American Scene* magazine. When he came into Rhymers Creek that day, a lot of the boys teased him pretty bad, and you could see people he didn't even know kind of pointing behind their hands and grinning at each other. All the rest of it Billy could've stood—all the money gone and the disappointment and even the broken heart.

What killed him was that everybody in the whole goddamn county had to know about it.

o o o

Billy Paul was one of those men who do not make an impression. He was not ugly or handsome, neither stupid nor smart. As a child, he had not been a bad boy, nor one who came to mind when people talked about a child who was especially good. In school he stoically made C's, usually did his homework, was never first picked for the baseball or football teams, but was not the last either. He collected a respectable number of merit badges as a Boy Scout—trailblazing and pioneering and water safety. It even appeared one year that he might go to the National Jamboree. But that didn't work out, and he dropped out long before he could have thought of becoming an Eagle. He had friends, though none perhaps who was ever a best one. A few times he went on dates, but rarely with the same girl twice. He had a crush once that remained unrequited.

He rode the yellow county bus each day from the little farm his family had between Olinda and what many people then still called Mockdon Parish rather than just plain Mockdon. His parents, Link and Mable, were gray country people whose own roots went back four generations in the county, though it's likely if you asked the Mortons or the Burneys or the Peters, who made such a show of being pioneers in the region, they probably wouldn't even remember who the Pauls were.

Billy's father died when he was nineteen, and Billy put himself to trying to run the farm. Two years after that, his mother had a stroke, was in Quiet Meadows Convalescent Hospital for three months, and died as well. After that, Billy let most of the land go fallow, though he kept some chickens and a truck patch with tomatoes and sweet corn and radishes and pole beans. He seemed to get by well enough working part-time in the Pep Boys stockroom, spelling Fred Bower on weekends and when he was too drunk to go to work. At Walgreens every so often, Billy picked up a men's adventure magazine or paperback and lived about as quiet a life as anybody in Mockdon County could imagine. He'd go see Fred from time to time, when he'd try and fail to get him to talk about 'Nam. About his only other friend was Ronnie Wallerby, who had grown up a couple of miles down the road and, even though he'd long before moved into Rhymers Creek, still came by the property about once a week just to check up. Beyond that, Billy Paul kept to himself, just a young bachelor getting older out on County Route 3.

I'd kind of look in on him and buy eggs. I like country eggs, fresh ones. The ones from the store always taste funny to me, and Billy's always tasted like the ones I remember from breakfast when I was a kid. He took real good care of his laying hens and he seemed real proud of them. Every time I saw him, I'd say something about it because that seemed like it made him feel good.

Billy was strange—I don't deny that. Not by constitution, but just by being alone. People get that way. Out there all by himself, he just turned kind of funny. Peculiar. Not ha ha. Not ha ha on purpose anyway.

We never talked about anything real important. It was always how his sweet corn was doing or a problem he was having with worms on the tomatoes. In the fall, he'd put up a lot of stuff. His momma had made him learn how to can back when he was twelve or something, which he never told anybody then because he was afraid they would think it was sissy. But he said he sure was grateful for it after, because it saved him lots of money, and home-canned produce was better than any of the processed stuff.

He had a television, but I don't think he watched it much. I'd try every so often to talk sports with him—about the Cowboys or the Jets or bowl games—but he never seemed much interested. Same way with the news. He'd bitch and moan about taxes now and then, but he never was much for politics either. He just drifted along like a piece of bark in a slow creek.

That's what I thought, at least. Then one day I was out there and I can't even remember now why it was, but we were shooting the breeze, and he went back to the bedroom to get something but since he was still talking I sort of followed along. I'd never been back there. Never had a reason to be. But anyhow, he was digging around and jabbering away and I was there in the doorway and, all of a sudden, there on the bureau, I noticed this picture. There were other ones—one of his momma, and her and his dad together, and one of him that must've been taken back in high school. But then there was this one all in color in a gold frame, bigger than all the rest.

It was of a girl.

And I mean, some girl.

I let out a little whistle and said, "Damn, Billy! Who the hell is she?"

He turned around and, just for a second, he looked real wild. But then he smiled—shy, you know—and said, "That's Alexandra."

"Where did you find her?"

He got flustered for a second, and then he said, "In Lemon Grove, last year. Remember I went up to that Antique Guns and Ammo show at the Quality Inn?"

I laughed. "Well, she's a hell of a lot more interesting than some old shotgun, I tell you. She live up there?"

"No. No. She's from California."

That made sense. Not too many Alexandras around Mockdon County, even these days when everybody gives their kids funny names. "She get out this way much?"

"No. It'll be another year at least," he said, "but we write lots of letters."

"Well, buddy, if I was you, I'd hightail it out to California real quick, or I'd get her back this way. And then I'd keep her under lock and key. Any woman that pretty'll have every red-blooded man and boy in this part of the state crawling through your windows to get at her."

Billy didn't like that one bit. You could see his face go cold just as quick as you sneeze. "Yeah, well, come on back out front," he said. "There's this article in *Real Adventure* I meant to show you."

Billy Paul was not really discontented, but he thought himself a coward. With only himself to take care of, he did not have to work that hard, and his wants, conditioned by a childhood in which there had always only been just enough, were simple. But he did feel, somehow, that his life now at thirty-two was very much as it had been at twenty-two and would be at forty-three or fifty-six or any other year up until he died. He read the paperbacks and articles in the adventure magazines, the stories of real men who defended their buddies and their country's honor, who made love to beautiful women and went in search of buried treasure and sunken galleons and lost cities. He knew he was not like that. Billy Paul was not made of the stern stuff of heroes. But even some little act, some small gift to the greater world—just that might be enough.

And, too, though he did not often feel it, he knew he was lonely, and that loneliness made him strange. He could tell from the way that Ronnie Wallerby looked at him sometimes. He'd say something, and Ronnie would get this expression on his face, and Billy knew that somehow he just sounded different from normal people.

That was why he never bought liquor. He had seen what liquor did to Fred Bower, who was strange, too, but had the excuse of having been to 'Nam. He would like to have somebody to share with. Even just a buddy would be all right, though Billy, when he thought of it, realized that what he really wanted was a wife. Even though he did not think of his parents as a couple particularly lucky, even especially happy, he remembered from time to time how his mother would stand at his father's shoulder as he laboriously reviewed the books yet another time, and she would gently stroke his hair as he tried to make the figures work yet again. He would recall his father coming through the door, still sweaty from the fields, smiling at his mother and singing some silly song he'd made up years before: "May-ah-ay-bel, she's got something on the tay-ah-ay-ble . . ." And then, in the dead of night, he would recollect the times, which he could count on the fingers of one hand, he had made love to a woman, though that was too polite a term probably, because in all but one instance, he had paid for it. And then it was as if, in the dark, an even deeper void opened up, and he wondered what he was living for at all.

Which was why, late one Sunday, thumbing through the latest *Real Adventure*, a certain advertisement was sure to catch his eye. *"BE A HERO,"* it said in bold letters, *"and give a beautiful young woman a new chance. She's young. She's pretty. And she's been abused: by fathers, brothers, husbands, unscrupulous Lesbians. But she's found a shelter with the Reverend George and Sister Faith in* The Congregation of Love. *Still, she needs your help. . . ."*

Under the write-up was a picture of a blond girl—smiling, scrubbed, stacked—and an explanation of the role and purpose of The Congregation of Love, founded 1968. Reverend George and Sister Faith took battered, raped, exploited girls with nowhere to turn into their "nonsectarian retreat high in the Santa Cruz Mountains of Northern California." There the girls lived a quiet life, full of meditation and communion with the earth. They were not nuns. They were simply taking time away from a world that had treated them shabbily. And they still loved men, though they were sheltered from them because of the traumas and shocks they had suffered. But, for an initial payment of only three hundred and fifty dollars, you could sponsor one of these young ladies to help defray the cost of her retreat. For that you would receive her photograph, and she would correspond with you. And, every two months, Sister Faith herself would send you a progress report to let you know how this "novice," as she called them, was progressing and how soon she would be able to reenter the larger world—"a complete and total woman, as if she were a virgin again."

Billy Paul sat there and looked at the photograph, hardly bigger than two thumbprints, of that beautiful blond girl, and he could feel himself getting hard—the first time in so long that he had not had to help himself along. Since the time he was a teenager, for lack of any stimulation he supposed, that seemed to happen less and less. Three hundred and fifty dollars was a lot of money, and yet, what else did he have to spend what little he had on?

Next day, he filled out the coupon, addressed the envelope, stamped it, and drove all the way to the central post office in Rhymers Creek to mail it so it would get there one day sooner.

o o o

After that one time, the time I saw the picture, Billy was always real private about Alexandra. I'd ask after her sometimes, kidding him, you know, but he never seemed to take it that way. You know how guys kind of razz each other where that sort of thing's concerned? But he didn't like it at all. He was real serious about it.

"Say, you hear from that lady friend of yours out in California lately?" I'd say.

And he'd look at me and kind of mumble. "Sure, just yesterday I got a letter."

"How's she doing?"

"She's fine."

"Headed this way soon?"

Then he'd get all tough-like. Billy Paul! He'd sort of stick out his chin and bunch his fists. "It'll be a while yet. But she's coming. She's making plans already."

Well hell—I mean, I never meant to rile him. But it was like he always thought I thought he was lying: that maybe he had met this girl who'd given him a picture up in Lemon Grove that weekend but that she was long gone. One Saturday, I'd been out to the property and caught my uncles, Elmer and Heck, snooping around. I told them to get their fat butts out of there or I'd kick 'em out and slap 'em with a lawsuit to boot. They've been after that land ever since my old man died, and I'll be damned if I can stand the sight of 'em.

But anyway, afterwards, I went by Billy's, and he was just happier than a fly in shit. He had a kind of bounce in his step and was whistling to himself when I got there, had the look around the eyes of a fellow who's won the Corvette at the County-Wide Chevrolet raffle.

So I said, "What's got into you?"

And he just smiles and says, "Oh nothing. Nothing."

"Bullshit!" I say. "I haven't seen you this happy since that brood-hen wandered up out of the woods that day. What the hell's going on?"

"I had a letter from Alexandra," he said. "She'll be here in six months."

"Six months! Jesus, Billy, we could all get blown to kingdom come in six months."

He looked at me like I was crazy. He wasn't about to let me ruin his good time. "Six months is no time at all. And she's re-virginized now. . . ."

"What?"

Then, all of a sudden, he shut down. His face just got all scared and mad and sad at once.

"Nothing," he said. "Re-surgeonized. She had a surgery. Nothing bad. She's gonna be all right."

Now, I knew I hadn't heard him wrong, and I thought maybe I ought to set him straight about certain things that are just the way they are where women are concerned. But it spooked me how he lost that glow he had. So I let it go. Maybe I should have pushed it.

But if you'd seen his face then, you wouldn't have done it either.

Dearest dearest Alexandra, he wrote. *The news you sent me makes me happier than I have ever been in my life. I know you will like it here. It is not California. But I have looked in Walgreens up in Rhymers Creek and they get many of the women's magazines you have talked about and also many other things for women. The lady at the cosmetics counter, Mrs. Rudolph, has been there for a long time and all the ladies in town say she knows more about makeup than anybody in the state. This is not a bad place. It will be very different from what you are used to but I know that you will be happy.*

The picture of you in your new dress is very pretty. I am glad you spent the $200.00 on something you wanted. I have not seen dresses like that here in Mockdon County but we are usually a little behind. Still everything does *get here with time so don't you worry! There is a dress store on The Square called Letting Loose that tries to keep up with all that is happening in New York and on the West Coast. Here is another $175.00 so you can buy yourself something else pretty. I like it when you use the money I send to get things that you like.*

Your last letter was wonderful but you do not have to be my love slave when you come here. I am serious about getting married. There is a pretty Methodist Church in Olinda I was baptized in and I think you will like.

The other picture I could not believe your friend got developed. I thank you for wanting me to see all of you but you really did not have to have Alice take it and take the chance that Sister Faith would find out and put you on probation. I have it hidden beside my bed and I look at it a lot believe me. I think of you always and I send you all my kisses and hugs—

I love you,

Billy

He looked at her letter again. Smelled the perfume of it. Alexandra. Beside him on the dining room table were the two photographs: her in a brightly patterned, shiny dress and her without any clothes on at all. He propped his chin in his hand and could not believe his good fortune. In weeks, she would be here. Alexandra, to share what little he had, willingly. She had said so. She had said, when she was growing up in Los Angeles, all she ever dreamed of was living in the country, on a farm, with chickens. And she always wanted to be out of the city, where people were hard and "deceitful." He was afraid sometimes she was so much smarter and worldlier than he was that he would bore her, but when he wrote that to her, she told him he was silly, that all she wanted was a man who cared for her, who was honest and worked hard like he did. She had had enough of those men who were "smart" and had sold her on the streets of Hollywood. She would not make the same mistake twice.

When he went to bed that night, he did not touch himself, though he wanted to. He kissed her picture on the bureau good-night and lay down, imagining what it would be like to have another body, warm and loving, there beside him.

So, six weeks ago, the shit hit the fan. I knew from the minute I got out of the car that something was wrong. The chicken coop was a mess, and Billy never let that happen. There was chicken shit all over the damn place, and the hens were pecking around in the yard, picking up the stray meal here and there because the feeder wasn't filled.

I went up and knocked and Billy didn't answer, but the door was unlocked, so I pushed on in. I yelled out, and there was nobody, so I headed back through the house and, finally, there in the bedroom, I found Billy.

He had the curtains closed, and he was on the bed, and there were papers all over the damn place. When I opened the door, he didn't even move, and there was half a bottle of Jack beside him. Billy'd never been a drinker, so a fifth of whiskey'd be enough to send him off to Timbuktu and back. The room was hot and closed and stank, and I thought, *Oh, we got a bad time here.*

Finally, he turned over and sort of squinted at me and said, "Jesus, Ronnie. What have I done? What the fuck have I done?"

I stood there a minute, and then that knowing came over me, that knowing where you say to yourself: *Well, son, something's gone real wrong here, and you're gonna have to take care of it whether you like it or not, so you better just get your ass in gear.*

So I said, nice and soft-like: "Well, Billy-boy, what's the story?"

"Look," he said, and I thought he was gonna cry. "Look."

He pushed two of the pieces of paper toward me, and I turned on the bed lamp so I could see better. He looked like shit. Pale, and with his eyes all sunk in.

I picked up the first one.

Dear Sir, it said. *I have discovered that Miss Alexandra Millis has sent you a photograph of an inappropriate nature*—now that, I thought, is something I'd like to see—*and so has been placed on probation. I hope you understand that we have Alexandra's best interests at heart and have determined that she should stay at The Congregation of Love for three months more than we had originally planned. . . ."* It was signed *Yours In Jesus,* Sister Faith.

That's not right exactly. But that's what it sounded like, you know. The real prissy, tight-ass kind of letter that just gives you a pain. But, of course, right then, I couldn't make heads or tails of it.

"Billy," I said. "What the hell is a Congregation of Love?"

His voice came out like somebody had him in a bear hug, all thin and high, like a little kid's voice. "It's where she lived. Where Alexandra lives. They were going to make her better there. She'd had a bad life, and they were going to make her better there."

"Who?" I said, "Who was gonna make her better?"

"Brother George and Sister Faith," Billy's voice started to quiver even more. "They'd take care of the girls and make it like they were like virgins again."

Well, you can bet I was smelling a rat as big as a Peterbilt, but it turned out I was getting there a little late in the game.

Billy pushed that other letter over to me.

I won't even try to quote it. It was one of those legal ones: "parties of the first part" and "parties of the second part," "defendants" and "complainants." What it came down to was one of those class action things. Guys in California and Oregon and Illinois and all over suing

The Congregation of Love for misrepresentation and breach of contract and who knows what the fuck else. All that law talk that makes us all crazy. And our poor old Billy, from the looks of him, just didn't know what to do.

I tried to think fast and put the best face on things, so I said, "Well, buddy, with all these high-powered lawyers on your side, looks like you can pick up some bucks here."

He stared. Just stared. And then finally he looked over at me and said: "Ronnie. Ronnie. There are two mortgages out on this property. Two mortgages. My daddy left me this land free and clear, and I owe the banks thirty-five thousand dollars."

"What the fuck!" I just blew up at him. I couldn't believe it. Billy? Old, boring, steady Billy. "Bill Paul. What the . . . What in God's name did you use thirty-five thousand dollars for?"

"Alexandra," he said real soft. "Alexandra. She had to stay there. They were going to make her well. And then she was going to come here." He leaned his face down in his hands. "Ronnie. They took me. They took me! I thought she loved me. I thought I was gonna have a wife. I thought everybody'd see then. But they took me! Oh, Jesus, what'll I do? What'll I do!"

Well, what was I supposed to come up with? I kind of grabbed hold of Billy's arm and I said, "You'll get it back. Talk to Sammy Stephens. He's an old bastard of a lawyer. He'll know what to do. You'll get the money back."

I knew that was bullshit, and I knew Sammy would tell him that, too, because he may be one strange fucker, but Sammy Stephens knows the law back-forward, and he'll always level with you even if it hurts. And just from the looks of that letter from the lawyer, I knew that a whole bunch of Billy Pauls were in just the same shape as mine was that afternoon, and they weren't going to see a red cent out of any phony cunt factory with Reverend Dick and Sister Puss out there on the West Coast.

Billy started to cry then.

I reached over and took him by the shoulders. "It's gonna be all right, damn it! It's gonna be all right! Cut it out!" I made him look me right in the eye. "They were just a bunch of motherfuckers! Bunco artists, you know."

And he just cried. "But I loved her, Ronnie. I love her."

o o o

The next several weeks, the last weeks of Billy's life, as it turned out, were quiet. He talked with Sammy Stephens, who took off the glasses he didn't like to wear and rubbed the bridge of his nose and said, "Oh, Billy. Billy. Billy. How could you believe these assholes?" Ronnie Wallerby took to dropping by every other day to take care of him a little. Billy wasn't eating, and not just Jack Daniels but about anything else at the liquor store helped to ease his pain.

The chickens fended more and more for themselves, and weeds began to crop up in the truck patch, strangling the radishes and smothering the marigolds that were supposed to keep snails out. Billy was at the point of giving up: humiliated and disillusioned and heartbroken all at once. Alexandra had not meant a word of it. It was only for his money. Seventy-five dollars here and a hundred dollars there and three hundred and fifty dollars a month for "maintenance" and the seven thousand dollars when she supposedly had the operation to make her a virgin again; then two thousand for Christmas so she could go on a shopping spree like she used to when she was a high-class call girl.

And he had not cared. Because it was only money, and it was only money that he could tenuously raise that seemed to offer him the chance to have someone beside him. So he had taken out the loans, at Greater Mockdon Trust and Rhymers Creek Federal and Mockdon Parish Bankers and Savings, not quite believing that they all did not know he was running himself into a debt he could never repay. But he could not quite believe it either, that for a photograph and a weekly, perfumed letter, he would wager all he had and all he had inherited for that pretty face from a state that might as well have been the moon, the face of a woman who promised to love him.

Then the other woman showed up. The one from the tabloid who somehow had uncovered the complaint and wanted to talk to the man from Middle America, the real victim, the saddest of them all. And he did talk to her, because Billy hadn't talked to much of anybody about it except Ronnie and Sammy Stephens, and with them he really didn't say all he had to say. Somehow it was easier with a woman, easier to tell her how Alexandra broke your heart, how you'd jeopardized everything you'd ever had in the world just so you could have a girlfriend, a wife, a companion whom you thought was coming from a dark past and so would not mind that you were poor and not very handsome and maybe not even all that bright. But you were honest and you worked hard and you were capable of love. And you thought that was what the Congregation offered you, because the advertisement for it appeared in a magazine that called itself "true," "real."

And the reporter was so empathetic, so moved by his plight, that he showed her the letters, the three boxes—the carbon copies of those he had laboriously written by hand as well as all her typed replies. She had read them. Dozens. And then, six weeks later, the words he had written to Alexandra, and those she had written to him, were on everyone's lips and burned into their memories.

It was the first time in his life he felt like people noticed him: poking each other and pointing and grinning. All he'd wanted was one person's attention. And instead, in Mockdon County, all over America, everybody had gotten a glimpse of his most secret heart, and they were laughing now. He knew that, if any of them had talked to that woman with the honesty and hurt that he had, their thoughts and dreams might seem just as silly or futile.

But they had not. And he had.

And now he would have to do something.

It was me who found him.

I'll damn the hide off him from now to my dying day, because he must've known I'd check by. He'd done a real good job on himself, I can tell you. It probably didn't take long.

He had her picture stuck in his shirt. Right against his heart, I swear to God. And I swear to God, too, if I ever meet the bitch, I'll strangle her with my bare hands and take whatever comes. And the same goes for that bitch from *American Scene*. I won't even tell you what I'd do to Brother George and Sister Faith.

It was all their faults, even if it was the magazine that killed him. That article even quoted—can you believe it!—some letters that reporter must've lifted while Billy wasn't looking, even though it was all agreed to by Billy's consent form from what Sammy said, because I made him write a letter, I was so pissed off. But they'd been real careful. Just what you expect from New York.

So Billy Paul's dead, and the banks own his place now, and from time to time I think of bidding on it because it's near my folks' property. But somehow, I can never bring myself to do it, because that land has a stink to it—a smell of lies and hurt and meanness.

Do you know what Billy said to me the last time I saw him alive, the very day he killed himself, after we'd all razzed him down there in Rhymers Creek? I should've known something awful was coming from that walleyed look he had, just before he got in his truck to go out to his place and end the whole damned mess.

He stood there, a little hunched over, and he said: "Ronnie. They just think I'm stupid. I've lived in this county all my life, and not much of anybody but you ever gave me a second thought. And now the only thing anybody'll ever remember is that I was stupid."

It's a sad state of affairs, if you ponder it. You gotta wonder what the world is coming to when a man thinks he has to kill himself because all he wanted was to be in love and instead ended up doing something dumb.

That day, he got back to the farm and put a little meal out for the chickens, which he had not done for two days. He brought the mail in—a couple of flyers and some credit card offer and a sweepstakes entry—and rinsed out the coffee cup he'd left that morning on the bureau.

It was not really something he had planned. He simply found himself later, with the stool from the kitchen and the rope in hand, beside a tree he seemed to remember, at a very early age, having watched his father plant.

And then, swinging the rope up over that limb had seemed just as natural as you please.

And securing that knot, something he must have learned in Boy Scouts.

Memento Mori

for Richard

Robert sprawled naked on his bed, writing in his journal.

Kirk could never keep a journal, not on this trip anyway. Maybe that's why he took so many pictures, even though pictures seemed second-best. On his own bed across the room, he cleaned the auxiliary lens with the special paper he'd brought from the States.

He was naked, too.

"What was the name of that street today?"

"What street?"

"Where we bought the blood oranges."

Kirk squinted. "I don't remember. I thought you wrote it down."

Robert reared up from the mattress, reaching for his jeans on the floor. From the pocket, he pulled a crumple of bus tickets and Metro tickets and match boxes and pesetas, spreading them on the sheet and pawing through them.

"Wasn't it some saint's name?"

Kirk nodded absently. "It was a woman's name."

"In this country, that means she was a saint."

They had visited the American girls in the room next door that night. There really hadn't been many Americans through the pensión in the two weeks they had been there. A Canadian couple stayed a few days, but they were older and standoffish and, like most Canadians in those days, all but had the maple leaf tattooed on their foreheads so as not to be blamed for what was happening in Vietnam. And besides, they were a couple and didn't need anybody to visit at night.

But the American girls were young, and when Kirk and Robert arrived with a bottle of cheap wine, they were glad to see them. The four had had a fine time with their maps, fingering where they had been and where they were going.

Back in their own room, Robert and Kirk had talked about the girls as they got ready for bed, peeling off stiff jeans and shirts and underwear sour with sweat, both a little groggy from the wine.

"That one was all right."

"Which?" Kirk said.

"Not Horsey. The other one."

"What's her name? Kat?"

"Yeah." Robert opened his journal. "I could dig rubbing her raw."

"Me, too."

The night before they had left the States, at Marcy's house, they had talked about buying a whore. The two of them together. They decided Paris was the best place. The Pigalle.

"I can't believe you guys!" Marcy was appalled. "If that's what you want, why don't you just go down on Fifth Street? There are whores here, too!"

"It's different," Kirk said, and Robert nodded.

"Oh, right." Marcy grimaced. "It's romantic."

They had not gotten laid since they arrived. They had met a lot of girls—an English redhead in particular they both liked very much.

Maybe that's why nothing happened.

Then there had been the two Spanish girls in Cuenca. Kirk and Robert started talking to them at the museum. Their names were Carmen and Pilar. From Seville. They were both blond.

The four of them visited the cathedral, bought stamps at the *tabacalera*, avoided the souvenir stands. They ate a cheap dinner. Afterward they went on a walk through the old stone city, separating slowly into couples. Robert and Carmen dropped behind. The moon washed the buff of the walls and streets, and Kirk took Pilar's hand.

She started to sing. Some children's song in a high child's voice. It made it seem there were somebody else there, not just an American boy and a Spanish girl. Kirk could hear someone else singing off in the distance.

He and Robert laughed about it back at the hotel, when they were getting drunk because they were horny.

They drank a lot, and often. Almost every night they bought a bottle of wine or bad cognac or dry anis. They spent a lot of time in bars with gin and tonics and *sol y sombras*, because it was different to drink at a bar, and they were still a year shy of legal in the States. Sometimes, when they had had a few, Robert would take out his journal—often in their rooms but even in the bars—and read from it.

"In the dark *tabernas*, they will tell you that *cuenca* means eye socket . . ."

Kirk smiled. It didn't really. It had once, but not anymore. Now it was something about a wooden bowl. That was what the bartender had told them.

". . . And it was true. They knew it. Things would never be the same again. But the poetry was always theirs, the moment passing from their hands—like the sun, brilliant and shapeless, in the noon Castillian sky."

When Robert read that aloud, Kirk had to cough before he spoke. Even then, the words came out pinched and rough: "That's really beautiful."

Robert grinned the catlike grin he did when he was excited or embarrassed.

"How much longer should we stay in Madrid?"

Kirk struggled with the new roll of film on the sprocket. "I don't know. Another couple days? When's the festival you want to see in Avila?"

"The fourteenth?"

He closed the back of the camera. "It's in that thing you picked up at the train station."

Robert raised up again, reaching beyond his jeans to the pocket of his backpack, his nakedness uncurling, lithe and sinewy.

Kirk watched, then put the camera to his eye and, without focusing, snapped the shutter.

Robert moved.

They looked across the room, from bed to bed—eyes troubled, uncertain.

"Oh, you flinched!" The chuckle wasn't real.

Robert cocked his head. "Do you want to try again?"

Kirk paused, then nodded.

Robert pitched forward, straining for his pack—a boy after a butterfly.

The shutter clicked.

They didn't say anything for a moment. Kirk fiddled with the advance and put the lens cap on.

He was blushing.

He smiled tentatively. "For when we're old."

He looked away.

"Do you want me to take yours?"

The air was suddenly hard and hot. Robert grinned like a cat.

Kirk gulped a breath.

"Yeah."

He set the camera down.

"Yeah. I do."

How the Coe Boys Got Their Names

for Annette

All that miserable August, she cursed Dr. Banfield, Del, love, her own plumbing, the U.S. Army, the United Nations, and Korea, both North and South. It was bad enough, in what everybody said was the sultriest summer since 1928, that she was into the eighth month of her first pregnancy. But then, six weeks before her due date, Dr. Banfield recommended a lying-in.

"With this kind of thing, Dora, we don't want to take any chances," he said while she was still up in the stirrups. "Besides, just think: what woman in your condition wouldn't want to spend a whole month in bed?"

A fat lot he knew about it! she thought. Flat on her back and covered with sweat, feeling like an overstuffed roaster in a slow oven. She really shouldn't complain, and, if Del were around, she probably wouldn't. If he were working down at his daddy's realty office, she could look forward to his being home at lunchtime and every night at five. And, too, she could count on his keeping his mother, his sisters, his father, the whole brood of her family, and the Millikins from next door at bay. But there in her third month, he had been called up and was now about as far away from Rhymers Creek as it was possible to be.

"Hell of a time for a war," he had grumbled the night they saw him off. Dora was trying to be brave there at the station, but, to her, the very word Korea sounded like it had four letters instead of five, even though Del assured her everything would be all right.

They walked slowly to the end of the platform, where he pulled her close, his hand wandering down to rest on her belly.

"Honey," he whispered, "there is one thing I want you to do."

"Oh, Del. Anything, anything."

"When this boy comes along . . ." He raised his hand to still her. He was convinced it was a boy. "When this boy comes along, no matter what my momma says, don't you dare name him after me."

She was a little startled at his vehemence. "But, honey . . ."

"No buts," he said. "I always thought Delmer was the stupidest name I ever heard—and by all the fights I had about it, I wasn't the only one—and I'll be damned if my boy's going to have to go through what I did over some dumb name."

"Well, okay, Del." She leaned tight against him. "Oh, Del, maybe it'll be a girl."

He kissed her. "It's a boy, Dora. I just know it."

Shiny as a basted hen on the bed, she'd sometimes marvel that she'd had no notion how difficult a charge her husband had laid upon her. It had really not been clear till after the lying-in began, when Momma Coe dropped by, resplendent as usual in an organdy dress, apparently unaffected by the humidity. White gloves, Dora noted with a mix of wonder and nausea: she was actually wearing white gloves!

"Honey, I've been meaning to get by these last two days and just haven't had a minute. How are you feeling?" Momma Coe prattled on about the heat, about a fashion show she'd helped organize for the Hillside Orphanage and one she was planning for the Red Cross, about Poppa Coe's latest siege with gallbladder. ". . . you know, we haven't had a letter from Del in what, two weeks now? Even if he is in Seoul, I just worry and worry. I know you do too, honey." She sighed. "It just seems so sad he won't be around when his own Little Delmer arrives."

For Dora, "Little Delmer" hovered in the air like a challenge, and she felt a sudden, swift kick inside her, as if her unborn boy was demanding she pick up the gauntlet and sally forth as champion of the infinite not-Delmers of the world. She reached for the magazine on the floor, the new *Saturday Evening Post*, as it turned out, and began to fan herself clumsily, staring off at a point just beyond Momma Coe's head.

"Well, Momma Coe, I don't know that we'd mentioned it, but Del and I've decided not to name the baby Delmer."

Momma Coe's face froze in a smile of impending mayhem.

"Why, no, honey," she said sweetly. "I mean, Delmer's been the name of the oldest boy in the Coe family for generations. It just didn't occur to me"—there was the slightest, growing tension in that voice—"that you would even dream of breaking a tradition like that."

"Really, it wasn't my idea." *The Saturday Evening Post* rose and fell. "It was Del's. I promised him before he left."

"Oh, the poor boy!" Momma Coe's voice had a vague edge of tears to it. "Poor boy, he was just beside himself then. You probably didn't notice, but I did." Here came the first sniffle. "You know he didn't mean it. Why, it would break his poppa's heart to do that."

Given that all of Poppa Coe's friends and relations called him Skeech, Dora doubted he'd be too concerned about the issue.

"All I've got to go on is what he told me," Dora said, "and he seemed pretty serious. As a matter of fact"—how could she be saying this? perhaps it was the heat—"he told me he thought Delmer was the stupidest name he ever heard."

Maybe it was Dora's imagination that transformed Momma Coe's little puff of outrage into the hiss of a small but extraordinarily venomous snake, but she was sure only Gramma Hutchins' fortuitous arrival saved her and her unborn baby from some unimaginably awful destiny.

"Yoo-hoo! Yoo-hoo! Dora!"

"Well." Momma Coe looked at Dora murderously as she straightened her gloves and stood. "I'll be getting along. But you better think about whether you want the responsibility for this. Just think about whether"—she was hissing again—"whether we need any more Franks in the world! Bye-bye." She sidled past Gramma Hutchins. "So nice to see you, Ethel."

Gramma Hutchins took up the station next to the bed. "What was that all about?"

"Oh, it's the baby." Dora sighed. "She's afraid I'm going to name him after Gramps."

"Well, you know." Gramma Hutchins settled back in the chair. "Franklin's a perfectly respectable name. Your grandfather was named after his uncle, who really was a pretty important fellow in his time. I think Frank always regretted we didn't name one of our boys Frank, and I've wondered . . ."

Dora felt a squirming inside that made her slightly queasy, as if the baby were trying to get his fingers around to plug his ears. She swallowed and closed her eyes.

"It really is a fine name, and, of course, there's Benjamin Franklin and Franklin Pierce—he was a president, wasn't he?—and it was good enough for FDR, so . . ."

This whole business was going to be worse than she had antici-
pated.

It was.

Over the next two weeks, the fury of the humidity and the rigors
of enforced idleness—even the bodily difficulties of that last month
of pregnancy—took a backseat to the battle that raged day in and day
out over naming the baby. It seemed like everybody—male and fe-
male, Del's blood kin and her own, old family friends, the next-door
neighbors, her chums from high school—had a great idea, the perfect
solution, the name to end all names. Dora's own mother pumped for
Lawrence, which she said always sounded aristocratic to her, while her
father mentioned his best buddy during World War I was named Seth.
Mrs. Millikin suggested Rudolph, which Dora told her sister she'd
gladly use if the baby turned out to be reindeer, to which Ellen replied
that she'd wanted to name one of her boys Beau, which meant handsome in French, and wouldn't it be nice to have a boy whose very name
meant good-looking?

"Sounds like a sure way to have a child with buckteeth and floppy
ears," Dora snapped, and Ellen didn't come back for two days.

That was better than Momma Coe, who refused to come at all,
though poor Poppa Coe got dragooned into the Delmer campaign,
showing up one night around nine o'clock to drone on about his grandfather and great-grandfather before him. Finelle Beauford dropped by,
full of her own ideas. Given her husband, Seedy, was named after Ce-
dric Hardwicke, Finelle didn't inspire much confidence either. Still,
Dora held her peace. She had made more than enough enemies in the
last few days.

Then she remembered something.

"Finelle," she said, "get me that dictionary in the front room. It's

Del's from high school. A Funk and Wagnalls maybe?"

With the tattered, blue cloth covers balanced precariously on her belly, Dora turned to the back, past the periodic table of elements, the Directory of American and Canadian Colleges and Universities, to the Glossary of Names.

Over the next several days, she tried them out on her tongue.

"Eugene Coe."

No. No, she thought, saying it aloud, "You! Gene Coe."

"Walter Coe."

Too much like a company, like some sign you'd see along Route 9. "Walter Co./The Finest in Plumbing."

Batholomew Coe. Ezekiel Coe. Hippolytus Coe. Rex "King" Coe. Oswald "Sublime Divine Governor" Coe.

Two weeks before her due date, Dora dashed off a desperate letter to Del: "Please, please, tell me a name that you like!" Half his people weren't speaking to her anymore, and her own family had turned decidedly crabby as the debate raged on. It seemed all the more unfair because her intentions were so serious. If her husband had left her the responsibility of naming that firstborn he was sure was a son while he himself was being shot at with rifles and machine guns and bazookas and whatever other awful Commie firepower the Russians were churning out to be shipped to those human-wave–attacking Chinese, then, by God, she was going to come up with the best, the most distinctive, the most exceptional name she could find.

As the days passed with stupefying slowness, however, she grew ever more desperate. Nothing she tried seemed right. Alexander Coe? Napoleon Coe? Dwight David Eisenhower Coe?

Then, one night, tossing as much as she was able with all that excess tonnage, wondering, too, if she were worrying the poor baby into brain damage, she hit upon a plan.

Dora took a sharp breath.

"Mom. Mom, I think it's time."

Her mother sat in the chair by the bed, working the crossword in the *News and Gazetteer*. "It's probably heartburn," she said soothingly. "You've got a week to go, and Dr. Banfield said his calculations were a little off. The first time, the baby's always a little late."

Dora felt another jolt.

"Mom!"

"Now, see. If they were contractions, they wouldn't come so fast. Lie still, honey. It's just some cramping."

Dora did as she was told. She began to feel light-headed in a way she'd never precisely felt before. Every so often, a flush would pass through her. Then came another stab, rolling down her belly like a wave.

"Mom! It's now. It's now!"

"Honey . . ."

"For God's sake, let's go!"

By the time her mother had called Daddy, who wasn't in, and then run to get Mr. Millikin next door, collected the suitcase that had been packed for weeks, put in a call to Dr. Banfield and another to the hospital, Dora had rolled out of bed and was on all fours on the floor, in the midst of a physical storm that seemed the bodily equivalent of the Revelation of St. John the Divine.

Mr. Millikin and her mother managed to get Dora to her feet and headed toward the door. Then, in some unanticipated flash of lucidity, Dora remembered the plan. She planted her heels stubbornly against the hardwood floor.

"Wait," she gasped. "Wait!"

They stood there supporting her on either side.

"Now. Now! Hand me that dictionary."

"What?"

"Don't argue with me, Mom. Hand me the dictionary!"

Her mother did as she was told, scrambling down beside the bed and pulling out the battered Funk and Wagnalls. With what strength she could spare from the moiling down below, Dora threw the book open and, despite an assault of nausea and double vision, stabbed triumphantly at the page before her.

"There," she said. "There! That is this baby's name!"

Her mother glanced at the place where Dora's finger rested.

"Now, honey, I think . . ."

"That's his name, damn it! Mr. Millikin. Mr. Millikin! What does it say? You are my witness. This is the baby's name. Now I want you to shout it out, or . . ." Another contraction nearly staggered her. "I'm not moving till I hear it. Shout it out, Mr. Millikin. Shout it out!"

He leaned over to see where she was pointing, on his face the look of a man utterly convinced that all women are, indeed, crazy. "All right, darlin'. All right. The baby's name is . . . ah . . ."

There was a long pause.

"You tell me! You tell me now. Aahhhhh! I'm not . . ."

"Okay, honey! Okay! It's . . ."

"Tulane?"

That was what Del said when the colonel called him into his office for cigars and congratulations that afternoon in Seoul.

It was only after he was back home that he heard about the plan. After trying again and again to make some kind of choice, Dora had decided to leave the naming in the hands of Providence, Fate, of that little fellow on his way out. When her labor started, when she still had the sense to think about it, she would simply ask for the dictionary, close her eyes, open the book to the Glossary of Names, and point to one—the one that was right.

And was it her fault that her labor came on so suddenly that she wasn't quite in her right mind? She really thought she'd found the page she wanted when she smacked her finger down. She hadn't been so far off. Only a couple of pages. But instead of the Glossary of Names, she was in the Directory of American and Canadian Colleges and Universities.

In S through Z, to be exact.

Del had laughed and pulled her a little closer. "At least you didn't get the chemical elements. We might have ended up with Uranium Coe."

"Or Arsenic Coe."

"Or Chloride Coe."

That set them to giggling so much that, as Dora later calculated it, that might have been the very night they conceived Wellesley, whose name she chose once again from among the Colleges and Universities. And so with Stanford, and with Oberlin, too.

Over time, Momma Coe convinced herself that it had all been her idea, and Dora's own people discovered in the family tree a Tremane and a Sanford, which allowed them to claim some heritage for the boys' names after all. Her sons themselves seemed satisfied, never confused with your average Toms and Eds and Larrys.

And Del—Delmer, the man she loved even if he did think his was the stupidest name he had ever heard—told her many years later that, if he had had any doubt about the choice he had made, Dora's wisdom in a time of trial had stilled it. Her ingenuity and fortitude when he found himself ten thousand miles away and fated to be a father was forever a reminder of love's good fortune too rare in the lives of men.

What Do You Do With Your Nights?

He lies on the bed.

She lies on the bed.

In the dark, she inhales sharply.

He smiles. "Why are women who smoke so sexy? I know it's bad for you, but there's just something about it that makes me hard."

"I'm putting it out." She breathes a laugh. "I don't want you to love me for my cigarettes."

"Oh, no," he whispers. "I love you because you wear panties to bed."

She giggles, then shivers at fingertips across her thigh. "It's always better when there's a little mystery. Remember when you wore your jockstrap?"

"We had fun that night. I don't think you ever came so fast." He shakes his head ruefully. "You made believe I was that quarterback. What was his name?"

"Funny," she murmurs after a pause, "I don't even remember."

A palm, ever so lightly, passes over his stomach in the dark, drops softly along his hip bone and squeezes his ass. He sighs.

"I'm going to kiss you now for all the things you did just for me, just because I wanted."

There is a warm tongue on her lips. Her mouth opens.

"All of it," he says. "Everything you did because I wanted to."

"But it was me. Me wanting. Ever since the first, I wanted you." She breathes. "I just had to hear your voice. You still have the sexiest voice I've ever heard anywhere."

He moans.

"Oh," she says, so softly he can barely hear, "you are hot tonight."

There's a begging in his timbre. "Just let me lick you. I want to lick you first. Everywhere."

"Yes. Yes!" She gives herself over to the feeling. She remembers the soft warmth of a mouth across her breasts, along her arms, on the backs of her knees. "Oh, please . . . please!"

She lets out a little squeal, and he starts to laugh.

"You're always so ticklish," he teases. "I can never get to the good parts before you get squirmy."

"You're terrible." She feigns a pout. "You are!"

"No, I'm not," he coos. "How're those panties? Feel my hand?"

A finger stretches the elastic. She gasps. It rustles through her hair, rests for an instant on her lips, and then, with a slow, circular motion, moves inside.

He groans. "Oh, you're wet already, aren't you?"

"Yes." She sighs. "Yes. All day. I've waited all day. At work, I could hear you. I thought about it at dinner. Online. Watching television. All the time, in my head, I was thinking of you."

He smiles. "Me, too." Against the sheet, he is so hard he can barely move without it hurting. "Please," he says. "I'm sorry. I have to now. I need you so bad."

"Do it," she says. "Please. Go ahead. I want you inside now. Please."

There is the throbbing grip like a heartbeat around him, and, slowly at first, he begins to pump, back and forth, back and forth. "Raise your legs higher," he whispers. "Raise up: I want you to take all of me."

"Yes." She pulls her thighs back. "Yes." She feels the thrusts go deeper, each one sweeping past that place that makes her shiver. "Yes oh yes oh yes," she sings.

"Oh, do you feel it? You feel so good."

"Yes. Yes. You always hurt a little, at first. But, oh, it's wonderful."

"Little girl. Little girl."

"Yes. Harder!"

"Oh, Jesus. Jesus!"

For a long moment, there is only their breathing—constant at first, then more and more ragged.

Then she says, "Can you see them? Can you see them?"

"Oh, yeah. Oh, yeah. Who is it? Who?"

"Raul," she says the name in two syllables. "Raul and Theresa."

"Oh, the brunette. The brunette with the tattoo."

"Yes. Yes, it's her. She's jealous. She's always wanted you. She can't stand watching, but she can't take her eyes off us."

"No. Really it's you she wants. She wants to make love to you. She wants . . ."

"She's going down on him. She has him all in her mouth, and he's watching us. He loves to watch us."

"Yeah. Yeah!"

"Be careful. Raul can hardly bear it. He's such a macho. And we know what his fantasy is. How many times has he tried now? He wants to be inside you when you're inside me. He's got his tongue back there now. Feel his tongue?"

"Yes. Yes! Oh, shit! I can't anymore. I'm coming. I'm going to come! I'm . . ."

"Yes. Yes. Go ahead. Yes! Now! I'll come with you. Yes . . . !"

"You're wonderful! Wonderful!" She laughs. She always laughs when she's with him. It's something that made them comfortable together from the first time they chatted. Neither was embarrassed or ashamed or at a loss for words. "It's not everyone who puts up with Theresa and Raul."

Now it's his turn to chuckle. "It was great you introduced us. They make me think about things I never let myself think before. Raul still kinda scares me. He's going to get me one of these nights."

"He will," she says knowingly. "But there won't be anything to worry about . . ."

There is a pause.

"Are you going to send that picture?" he asks.

A beat.

"No." She sighs. "No. I've really been thinking about it. It's better that we just imagine."

He sits up, swings his legs over the edge of the bed. The magazine beside him rustles, falls to the floor.

"I guess you're right. But, you know, hell, men are scopophilic."

"What's that?"

"They get off with their eyes."

"Oh." She nods to herself. "It sounds so dirty! But still, you do a pretty good job with your ears!"

"I guess so." It's his turn to sigh. He rests his chin in his hand. "You know, years ago, people didn't have to do this."

She shrugs. "That's so long, I barely remember."

He hesitates. When he finally speaks, there's a hint of nervousness in his voice. "I'll do the call tomorrow night. You'll be off-line by then?"

"Sure." She giggles. "I'll be watching Letterman. I think he's a dweeb, but what do you do with your nights?"

He nods his head slowly and shifts the phone to his other hand.

"Yeah," he says wistfully. "What do you do with your nights, after all?"

Peach Queen

for my father

He came when he was called, though wound in the blankets and ready for sleep. His father's voice rose, low but insistent, as the boy groped to the door, not sure the words he'd heard were real. Thumping down through the half-dark, he could see his father at the foot of the stairs, arms akimbo, his great, red beard covering the cleft of his collar. Lin shivered as he emerged from shadow to light, squinting his eyes against the glare.

"What is it, Daddy?"

"Want to go down to see the train?"

"Which one?"

"The Peach Queen."

"I guess." Lin bugged his eyes. "It's late."

"Oh, not too late." His father smiled, turned the boy around, and gave him a pat on the bottom to send him upstairs. "Get your clothes on."

Dressing in the dark, he was careful to be quiet so as not to wake his little brother, who was rolled shapeless in the covers of the lower bunk. His legs whispered into his jeans. He unlaced his shoes to slip into them instead of stamping them on. Thrusting his arms into his wool shirt, he jarred the bureau. The Big Ben clock, ticking softly, slapped forward on the wood. The boy jumped and glanced over at his brother, who did not stir. Relieved, Lin righted the clock, not looking at the face.

He crept to the window to judge the night. The pines clustered thick, blacker than the starred sky, still and secret in the windless dark. The ground shimmered pale, and the promise of snow seeped through the glass. On the way out, he pulled the toboggan his mother had knitted onto his head and picked up his peacoat.

"Ready?"

"Uh-huh."

"Let's go then."

His father zipped his jacket, the leather one from the War. His pipe poked out of one pocket; the other bulged with a timetable and a newspaper clipping.

The cold outside was brittle, and the brown grass crackled under Lin's shoes. In the car, it did no good to use the heater at first, so he pulled his knees up beneath his chin, grasping his legs against the chill.

He knew he would be tired next day at school.

At first they did not speak, rolling through the neighborhood to the boulevard that led downtown. They turned down the street where the rich people lived in their brick, be-columned houses, the old families whose children went to private schools and got fast cars when they turned sixteen.

"Why are we going to see the train tonight?"

"This is our last chance," his father said, lighting his pipe as they waited at a traffic light. "They're pulling it off tomorrow."

The car filled with the sharp smell of tobacco. Lin watched the smoke curl up from the bowl and steam from beneath his father's mustache. Always when they went to the trains, his father brought his pipe, even on the stagnant summer nights when the two of them—sometimes with Lin's mother and sister and brother—drove down to the station to see the Peach Queen. On Sundays, they might go in the afternoon to see the Crescent arrive. But though the Crescent was a grander train, with twelve silver cars and a round-end observation, it was not touched with the same magic as the Peach Queen, hurtling from night into night, dark stream across a dark land, crying lonely against the black.

"When did you hear?"

"Hear?"

"About the train."

His father fished in his pocket. "It was in the paper." He laid the clipping on the seat.

"Why are they taking it off?"

"Just doesn't make money anymore."

As they drew nearer the center of town, there were fewer trees. Lin leaned his head against the window. The tight, white bungalows of the mill workers floated past—clapboard clouds in the starlight, all shrubbed the same. In them lived boys who smoked on the sly, Baptists who called someone they disliked a Jew. Lin thought of them in class: tough, foulmouthed, keeping to themselves. They read badly and figured worse, but he envied them secretly, for their mothers let them wear jeans to school. He wondered if they knew about the train, if their fathers had ever taken them, even before they could really remember, down to the tracks to watch the limiteds flash by. Sitting in the car, staring past the mill houses to those times half out of mind, Lin heard the diesel engine howl and the cars moan and felt the scruff of whiskers before the cushion of the beard as he pressed his face in happy fear against his father's cheek.

The streets downtown were bright, and, behind plate glass, displays of clothes and toys and appliances were spread out for no one to see. They passed a lone policeman sauntering down the sidewalk in front of the Presbyterian Church, its graveyard neat beyond the streetlights. Approaching the tracks, the Milner Hotel loomed before them, four squat stories of brick, home to retired engineers and brakemen and gandy dancers, their loneliness broken, perhaps, by the companionship of others who had labored as they had labored and the rumble at all hours of the trains.

They parked by the station.

"There won't be any more trains at night after this, will there?"

"The Crescent comes through going south at four."

"Maybe we can come down and see it."

His father laughed. "I don't think you'd do too well at four in the morning."

Inside, the steam pipes clanked, and the chandeliers—their bowls gray with dust and dead moths—burned bravely but a little futile against the dark. The room smelled stale. On one of the wide, swart benches sat a colored woman in a blue coat and hat, eyes liquid and old. At her side were two children, both younger than Lin, dozing as they waited for the train. Glancing at them, Lin stumbled on a worn place in the floor. He looked quickly away, up beyond the chandeliers to the faded, shadowed ceiling.

"Do you want some timetables?" his father asked.

"Sure," Lin said, and they walked to the ticket window.

The stationmaster, gray-haired and bespectacled, rubbed his hands together over the radiator. Beside him hung an old mahogany clock, its pendulum rolling hypnotically back and forth, across its top a shiny brass plate that read "Southern Railway" in curled and sloping letters. To its right was the timetable rack.

Lin's father tapped on the lathe bars of the ticket window.

"Yes, sir," the stationmaster said.

"Thought we'd get the young man here some timetables."

"Okay." The old man waved toward the rack. "Which ones do you want, son?"

Lin squinted across the office, trying to decide. The harsh light made it difficult to make out one from the other. He settled on a B&O, a Monon, and an Erie-Lackawanna.

As the stationmaster handed them to him, he said, "Now, you be sure to save these, son. Maybe someday they'll be worth something." He shook his head and looked at Lin's father. "We get less every season."

"Yeah. And they get thinner and thinner."

The old man slouched casually against the counter. "Well, sure. They take off more and more trains every day. Not just locals anymore either. No more Columbian. And the Rockets and the 400s, most of them gone now, too." He shook his head theatrically. "And here we go tonight, with the Peach Queen making her last run."

The men were silent for a moment.

Lin shifted his weight. His father spoke.

"Imagine you're pretty low about that."

"Oh, yeah. Yeah." The stationmaster nodded heavily. "Takes some getting used to every time. Sometimes, you know, I think I should have stayed with the Pennsylvania."

"You were with the Pennsy?" Lin's father said.

"Yep. Been twenty-five years ago now. During the War."

"I was with the Pennsy Pittsburgh. In 'forty-six."

"In the yards?"

"Yeah."

"Say, you might have known my brother-in-law . . ."

Lin settled onto one of the benches, rolling his shoes on the heels, studying the timetables. He had heard the stories about the Pennsylvania before. There were steam engines then. His father told him about them and showed him pictures: Limas and Baldwins and Pacifics. Lin did not understand. They must be very different from diesels, he thought, though he could not tell exactly how.

One of the children awoke and whined. The old woman hushed him. Lin wondered if she was their mother or their grandmother. Occasionally she leaned forward, her face in her hands, as if asleep or crying. Lin put his elbows on his knees. Were they going somewhere, or were they meeting someone? If they weren't taking the train, he thought, it was very late for the children to be up.

Maybe something had happened.

Maybe somebody was coming home.

"Come on, Lin. Let's get out on the platform."

His father had gotten a drink from the bubble fountain. There were droplets of water in his beard.

They went back to the cold night, barely broken by the naked bulbs hanging from the platform canopy. Lin strained both eyes and ears against the black to catch the shimmer of the headlight or the moan of the horn. Around them there was the clatter of preparation: the voice of the stationmaster and a baggage cart rattling the brittle silence. They waited a few minutes.

Then, far down the track, they could see it—a speck growing slowly in the night—and hear it—a high, thin ghost of a sound half-lost, echoing each time louder.

Lin's father suddenly was not beside him but trotting down the platform, one hand in his pocket. He stepped onto the tracks and knelt.

Afraid for an instant, Lin raised his arm, "Daddy!" But then his father was with him again.

They stood together, their faces both grave and excited, sharp-shadowed in the glare. The horn howled as if to cover the whole scale of notes, and the light whirled drunken, spinning its rays to break the night.

The air shook.

The train came.

It rolled into the station: two units and four cars made grand by the din and the dark, past man and boy at trackside. Lin took a step back, unwilled, as the engine, then the cars, loomed over him. The clack slowed, then stilled, and the brakes hissed not like a cat but like a man exhausted. The conductor stood in the Dutch door of the last car, a Pullman called Guilford Court House. The train gave one last groan of a live thing, then stood as if asleep. From one or two of the dark compartments, bleary faces pressed the windows, eyes slitted against the light. The thump of luggage bouncing clumsily against the walls came from the vestibules. Lin's father walked to the end of the train, the boy following.

"Take a good look," his father said, motioning toward the illuminated masthead. "This'll be the last time you'll see it."

Lin gazed long at the sign, trying to fix in his mind the yellow-and-rose–colored fruit crowned with the legend "The Peach Queen" in script, all brightly lit by bulbs half-visible through the frosted glass. "The last time," his father had said. "The last time." Lin thought of the steam engines, of a lost and incommunicable magic he could not understand, and knew then, striving to etch the sign in his boy's memory, that the Peach Queen tonight disappeared and could never again be comprehended as before but must exist as a story, a memory, a dream recounted but never recaptured.

Embarrassed suddenly that he might cry, he looked away, up the platform, and saw them: the children and the old colored woman. Her head down, she shuffled as if movement itself grieved her. The boy and girl followed, fidgeting to hurry.

Lin walked closer.

The old woman raised her arm in greeting, and, from within, there was a rustling. Down from the vestibule stepped a younger woman dressed in black, her brown cheeks warm in the glow of the harsh lights. The old woman embraced her, then let go and held her with her eyes.

"Buried?"

The younger woman nodded nervously, quickly, then knelt to take the children in her arms.

The old woman shook her head, speaking in a still, sad voice. "Oughta never left. Never. Never in this world."

The younger woman stood, whispering, "Not now, Mama."

They huddled together, speaking low.

Then they began to walk, the old woman saying: "We oughta all get on. Right now. Get on and ride down to Elkins. Elkins is where we belong."

And the daughter, a child at each hand, softly: "No, Mama. Ain't no trains to Elkins anymore."

A hiss rose, then three short barks as the engine awoke. Lin felt his father beside him and heard the conductor's shoes clang on the metal steps of the Pullman.

"All aboard!"

The horn sounded, bellowing now, and a rumble rose as the couplers strained. Very slowly, the wheels turned and the cars crept forward, almost imperceptibly. Then they threw their weight behind the locomotive, and, with a squall and a rattle, the train began to roll. The bottom half of the Dutch door slammed shut, and the conductor, as he passed, waved good-bye. The train gathered speed, the noises blending gradually into one.

Then it was gone.

Lin and his father looked down the tracks, watching the luminous peach fall away. They waited long in the night, the two together. The platform was deserted, and Lin, struck suddenly lonely, moved a step closer to his father. The silence was so complete, Lin could hear the ticking of his father's watch.

"Hold on."

Lin watched as his father hopped down onto the tracks and walked, counting his steps, eyes riveted to the ground. Finally, he knelt and struck a match, then probed the ballast with his fingers. He came back to where his son stood and opened his clenched hand.

"Here."

In his palm were two pennies, pressed flat by the train.

"You take one, and I'll take the other, and we'll both have something to remember the Peach Queen by."

Lin picked up one of the shiny slabs of copper, warm from the train and his father's grasp. He looked at the man's face.

"Thanks, Daddy," he said in a voice not quite his own.

The train was gone. The darkness threatened. The only sound was the heartbeat tick of the watch on his father's arm.

In the lights of the platform, Lin noticed—for the first time—a fine, gray weave amid the rust of his father's beard.

Wonderful Town

for Jean Oliver, and for my mother

Judy was a little jealous of Jean, she had to admit. She, after all, was the one who had always wanted to go to New York.

Chicago was fun, of course. She'd been going there with her mother since she was a girl, and she and Jean had gone a couple times the summer after high school. She had applied for jobs in the city a few weeks before and was hoping the one at that insurance company would come through.

Still though, Jean made New York sound endlessly more glamorous.

Jean's joining the WAVES wasn't that much of a surprise. Everybody wanted to do something for the war effort, but beyond that, the WAVES were likely to get her farther away than any other option, which was what Jean was most interested in. If things at home, for Judy, had been a little spare—given the Depression and all—for Jean they were not just spare but ugly.

They never talked much about it, but Judy knew.

Jean's first letters trilled with the sheer excitement of Manhattan. If Chicago teemed with soldiers and sailors, Judy could only imagine what New York was like. In Chicago, they were training up at Great Lakes or Glen View or one of the countless other bases scattered around the city, but in New York, they were all converging to make the trip across the Atlantic, off to England or North Africa or on to Italy.

"There are cute boys everywhere!" Jean gushed. "FROM everywhere!"

She'd had dates with fellows from Florida and Maine and New Mexico and Oregon; San Luis Obispo and Nashville and Helena and Charleston, West Virginia. An ensign from Savannah had taken her to dinner at the Waldorf-Astoria, and a major from Wyoming got them tickets for *Oklahoma!*

Jean said it was the most wonderful play she'd ever seen.

Stuck in Galesburg, Judy could only imagine. The touring company would come to Chicago, of course, but that wasn't the same as seeing it on Broadway.

Jean'd done all the tourist things—the Statue of Liberty, the Empire State Building ("You really can see three states, and if it's really clear you can see four!"), St. Pat's, and Rockefeller Center. She'd been out to Coney Island endless times on the subway and even had gone way uptown to see Grant's Tomb (he was from Illinois, after all) and St. John the Divine ("They're not even a quarter done with it!"). The Bronx Zoo. Madison Square Garden. Christopher Street. She'd been to the Broadway Canteen so many times, she couldn't count.

Of course, there was also work—typing and filing and running messages all over town as ship after ship was loaded up with men and then headed east.

o o o

From the first, Jean told Judy to have the boys from town who'd been called up and were headed that way to look her up. She was always game to show them around, though she admitted, by her twelfth trip up the Empire State, she getting a bit jaded. "I was exhausted when Lenny and Fred came in, but I did my best to be perky," she wrote. "I told them that was Pennsylvania way off west even though I think it was too hazy to see that far. Probably just more Jersey! But they were both so cute in their sailor suits! I can remember when they were just kids. . . ."

After the first six months or so, the letters were fewer. Judy had gotten the insurance job in Chicago and had moved there. Still, she went home pretty much every month, so she got news of Jean from their mothers, though even they said she wasn't nearly as communicative as she'd been when she first got there.

"Well," Judy said in Jean's defense, "she's made friends. She's not homesick anymore." She always had been a practical person. "I'm sure things are getting busier than ever." Everybody knew the invasion of Fortress Europe was coming. "Besides, the novelty's worn off now."

Living in a big city, she thought herself more worldly than she had been before, more aware of just how vast everything was—especially this war that now sprawled across the entire globe: from Africa to India to China, to Russia and then back to Italy.

Her mother remarked that Sam Atkinson and Ronnie Tyler had tried to get ahold of Jean before they shipped out, but she'd told them she was sorry, that she was working at the Navy Yard now in Brooklyn and so was stationed out there and didn't get to the island much. The same happened when Buster Lynde shipped out, then Walter Coughlin and Giovanni Manfreddi.

In the meantime, Judy met that navy aviator on the train. To say it was a whirlwind courtship was an understatement, or would have been if times were normal. But they weren't. She'd wanted Jean to come to the wedding, but she couldn't get leave.

Then she and her new husband were off on their own peregrinations to Corpus Christi and Jacksonville and Falmouth and Cape May and then to Alameda. Endless journeys on endless trains. Sometimes, the two of them would poke their heads out the window or the Dutch door to try to see the last car, and a lot of times, they couldn't.

They did pass through New York now and then, but it was just to change trains. She talked to Jean on the phone from Penn Station.

She sounded tired, Judy thought.

Back home, pregnant, her new husband off on a carrier somewhere in the Pacific, Judy heard Jean had gotten leave to come back for a few days. Her dad's cancer was terminal, and he wasn't expected to last much longer. Judy told Jean's mother to tell her come by when she needed a little break, that she'd love to see her. She herself was big as a house, and getting around wasn't all that easy. She kept busy writing her new husband every day, along with letters to a couple guys he told her never got anything at mail call. She'd just chat in those notes about the weather and new movies and *The Goldbergs* on the radio, but her husband told her it meant the world to them.

The third night after Jean got back, she dropped by. The two of them looked at each other.

They had grown so much older in such a short time.

They talked about Judy's wedding, about her whirlwind tour of America, of what to name the baby; about Jean's various duties—and varied they had been—as a WAVE. And then later, more tentatively, about a couple of affairs Jean'd had and of a proposal she'd thought long and hard about before rejecting.

Eventually, Judy felt she had to bring up Giovanni, about how his mother was disappointed that Jean couldn't get away to show him around. After all, both she and Judy had always been so tight with Gina, and Gio was her favorite brother.

They were on the back porch, smoking. Neither of them had smoked two years before—well, not often.

Jean took a deep drag from her unfiltered Spud.

"After a while, Judy, with the boys from home, I just couldn't." Jean looked long into the night. "I just couldn't."

There was a long pause, and a chill passed through all Judy's pregnant body.

Judy realized Jean was crying.

"They all died," she said simply. "They all died."

Traveler

for the Craigs

You gotta pace yourself.

With anything, I guess.

And the highway's there. On and on and on.

With the state police and the highway patrol and the local cops and ladies with cell phones and who knows who the fuck else, you gotta make it quiet.

You gotta take it easy.

And keep an eye out for the others.

They're on the highway, too.

For alla 'em, you gotta make it look like you're just the most respectable fucker on his way home. Just a hardworkin' family man. Maybe out for a little fun. Rollin' down the road, I want nobody to give me a second look.

Years back, a couple years after my tour was up, I cut my hair. It was past my shoulders then. But, now, I wear it close to the scalp. Not too close—that looks weird, too. No beard. No mustache. No identifying marks.

You gotta lead 'em gentle.

I always wear a nice shirt, too.

I won't explain the liquor. It's what I use. I'd buy other stuff, I guess—dope, acid, crank—but I'm too old and lonesome. And I never stay no place long enough for a connection.

And drugs make you careless.

And stupid.

Four Roses. Polski vodka. Old Crow. Those boys're always just down the block, just up the street or around the corner, anywhere you go.

I drive.

Just when I have to.

When it's time for a mission.

Mostly I stay home, wherever that is, and listen to country and classic rock and go to bed with the chickens. Days I put in cabinets and replace shingles and frame doors and install new decks on the backs of little houses in Wyandotte or Fountain Valley or El Paso or Buttfilly, Kansas.

I never know when.

I see something in a magazine. Hear a song on the radio. There's a fire.

It's just time.

They come outta my insides, and when they're filled, they go back again way deep inside me, as if they never were at all.

At first, it was a year. Even two. Then the wars started again, and they started comin' round more often. They just tell me it's time, and I gotta hit the highway. Travel for days. One state. Two states. Three states. Five.

I get so tired.

And the others?

They don't resist.

They got no chance to resist.

They don't know they oughta resist before it's over.

If you know how to drink, how to pace yourself, then you can drive forever—till California sinks into the ocean, till every place you ever thought you remembered disappears—and you are just that guy on the road every boy dreamed he'd be someday.

It's just you and your traveler tucked under your seat, keeping you company. Keeping you steady. Keeping you sane.

And them, of course. Pushin' out of the ash.

It makes you all excited and bored at once.

Always there's the highway. Tres and the highway.

There will always be the highway.

And there will always be Tres.

And those times you understand all kinds of things you didn't before, or that you did once but forgot or goddamn wish you had. Burned 'em up till there's nothing left but ash. Blown away by the wind you make when you're drivin'.

You wish!

But you know where you're comin' from and you know where you're goin'. Not the places, exactly. But that space in your head, in his head, in her head, in Tres's head, in God's or the Devil's who gave you your mission—that space. That place way beyond what any real space can be. That's when I know who I am and what I have to do.

I'm an angel.

Tres told me.

I'm an angel.

You know how it ends. I have to save them. For him, and for me. Every one of them I can.

When I drive, I think of Tres. Every time.

I'm headin' down 80 or 75 or 101. I'm drivin', and I'm drinkin', and it's night, and the black is heavy and deep and shiny-strange as Tres's skin, stars like the sweat on his cheeks and his shoulders. He's there—all smart-ass and sassy, all no-shit-from-no-man. We both nineteen. Sleek and slick and skinny and full of everything a boy should be at that age—just by accident sent straight to hell.

At first, we hated each other. Me his peckerwood nightmare, and him, that thin city nigger who just showed we shoulda kept 'em down on the plantation and beat their asses every day and twice on Sunday. How we got assigned to the same platoon was some pervert's dream.

It took time. The guys had to pull us off each other more than a couple times.

I'm gonna fuck you up, you honkie-bitch mothafuck!

You lazy-ass Sambo! Suck my fuckin' dick! ·

And then it was pushes and shoves and fists and kicks and the other guys yellin' *Cool it, you dickheads!* And all those hands all over us draggin' us apart. *You'll get us all fucked, you assholes!*

But slowly, slow, we took to each other. We saw each other real—me that slummy peckerwood and him that ghetto nigger. I don't remember when I figured out he was just as scared as me. Not of the towelheads. No. It was the other guys: the sergeant, the officers. All the fuckers who were better. The ones who knew their daddies. Who didn't get fucked up the ass by the big boy next door or the priest at church when we were nine or ten. Who sat in school and felt stupid. Who joined up because that was the only fuckin' way we'd ever get out of the nasty places we came from.

The ice picks come from the dollar store. The wire comes from Tru-Value. They always end up on the shoulder or pitched deep in some slough or crick miles and miles from where it happened.

I just buy more when it's time.

Tres and me. We were buddies. I knew by then he'd die for me, and I'd get gangfucked with razor wire for his black ass, and he knew that, too. We'd get stoned. We'd get drunk. Snort. Tweak. At the base in the States, we'd go out in a field and get shitfaced and laugh at all the stupid fucks down at the bars in town gettin' wasted and hopin' some poor little pussy would take 'em out back in the alley. We'd giggle like girls at those hopeless shits. We were Cheech and Chong. We were Robin and Superboy.

We didn't give a flyin' fuck about America or the army or whatever the fuck we'd gotten ourselves into.

I think of Tres a lot.

But only on a mission.

The missions are hard. They're for Tres. For all the Treses. For me, too. Because I don't want those boys out there. Goin' crazy like we did. Those good boys'll go back to good homes where they'll try to be good. Those good girls, too, these days.

But they'll never be good again.

They'll have the ash people, deep down inside, and maybe those fuckers go to sleep ten or twenty or thirty years.

But they come out sometime.

And all hell breaks lose.

Me and Tres, the two of us, we were never worth a sweet goddamn. But we were made to save 'em. Every one we can.

And he's dead.

And I'm not.

So I do what I have to do.

Most of the time, day to day, I'm easy. I just build things. When I was a kid, the man next door, Mr. Longley, taught me. He felt sorry for me. He had a lotta tools, and when he was makin' a bookshelf or a cabinet or a desk, he'd ask me to come over and help. I was no fuckin' help and when I got to be fifteen or so, I hated him 'cause he did feel sorry for me and I knew it and he knew that I knew.

But he was good to me.

I don't care about the sorry anymore.

I feel sorry for the ones I meet up with.

But I know I'm doin 'em a favor.

Just like Mr. Longley did for me.

On a mission, I look for 'em at the malls, on the strips, at the rest stops. *No one will ask. No one will want to know.* From Oregon to Alabama to New Jersey to Arizona, they will never put it all together.

The broken neck.

The stab wound to the skull . . .

I studied it. I bought the books the doctors buy. The ones for the criminal justice classes.

Sure, me and Tres had those stupid bayonet drills. Apeshit stuff. "Blood! Blood! Blood!" Drivin' good boys to kill.

What did they know?

Tres and me. We were born killers. But because we were, after what we saw, after goin' to hell, we were ready to save 'em.

And since Tres ain't around, it's up to me.

After the highway, after Tres was dead, I hung out when I could with special forces. Fuckin' dildos. Crazy fuckers. I hated their fuckin' guts. College boys, ex-jocks, psychos.

Mostly, I just listened.

And when I got out, I went to the branch library to look things up.

"Garrote."

"Spinal cord."

"Asphyxia."

I don't want no one to suffer.

I just want to make sure they're dead.

Me and Tres.

They ended up hatin' us both—smart-mouth dicks from nowhere. All those pussies who went into the service so they could go to college or who came from college, even though they all were the same poor mouth, sad-ass, white boy/black boy trash we were.

That's what me and Tres loved in each other: that we were scum already. Just scum tryin' to make the best of it. Black? White? Brown? Yellow? Tan? Blue?

Who the fuck cared?

We'd look each other in the face, and it was just lookin' in the fuckin' mirror.

By the time we got to Kuwait, it was almost over. Tanks blastin' up toward Bagdhad. Sad-dam shittin' in his fuckin' boots. The air was ugly with smoke, and it hurt to breath from what the Republican Guard had blown up. Oil wells like hell—spewin' shit.

Tres and me laughed.

"Shit, man!" He'd smuggled some 'shrooms in. "Looks like the fuckin' hell Father Smathers told me about."

"That when he had his dick up your ass?"

"Slam yo' ass!" He giggled.

We giggled a lot with all the drugs.

It was great duty.

"Okay, dudes, you're doing graves patrol."

It got all quiet for a minute.

"What the fuck is that, Sarge?" It was Bowman, one of the college boys.

Sarge didn't say nothin' for a minute. Then he said, "They made a big mess on a highway up north. We got orders to clean it up and keep it quiet."

"What the fuck, Sarge!" Linder. He was another college boy. "What's this shit about keepin' it quiet!"

"Don't give me lip, Linder!" the Sergeant yapped. "We got orders. That's it!"

It was only later they called it the Highway of Death.

They were retreating then—Republican Guard, drafted punks, Kuwaiti collaborators, electricians from Basra, mechanics from Mosul. Brothers from Falluja. Daddies from Anbar.

I never seen nothin' like it.

Napalm and phosphorous.

Thousands.

High explosives.

More than thousands.

Close and crowded.

Crispy chickens.

Cinders and ash.

All of them screaming.

"My shittin' Christ!" Bowman whispered.

They made us dig graves.

A lot of graves.

I just bit my lips, threw sand like it was magic fairy dust. It stank. Like burnin' meat. Like your face shoved into a charcoal grill. Either that or the sweet shit smell of rot, rot, rot in a hot, hot sun, and it was hard to tell which was worse.

But worst was the burnt-up faces, the burnt-up crotches and butts and hands, those burnt-up chests and backs and no-toes feet. Those burnt-up nothin'-that-was-left and thinkin', "Jesus, shit! He's me!"

We pitched 'em in. A thousand? Couple thousand? A thousand more. *Carbonized:* that's what the medics said. Like cheap briquettes. Like Labor Day. You picked 'em up, and they came apart. Their legs fell off. Their heads went south. You grabbed an arm, and it went to pieces in your hand.

Tres started to puke.

Just sudden.

He didn't have much in his stomach, so it was bile and dry heaves. And he couldn't stop. It was like that charcoal-face Iraqi kid was his goddamn brother.

It went on and on.

"Dude!" I said. "Dude! It's okay. Don't freak! It's fuckin' okay! Just stop!"

But he couldn't.

He just kept pukin'. Till he made blood.

It was so goddamn ugly.

It was goddamn ugly.

Don't believe what they tell you.

It was thousands. And thousands. Blown to pieces. Burnt alive. Charred faces with their lips burned off so those fuckers were smilin' like zombies in the movies when we had to pry their sorry asses off the tanks and the APCs and the trucks and the cars and the cycles and the bikes off the side of the road and then throw them into the pits we dug. Pick up an arm. Trip on a foot. Look at that tank driver's scream as the fire shoots up from below and fries him in five seconds and there just ain't time to get out.

But there was five seconds when he knew. . . .

And you knew that, too.

It was that one day, and the next, and the next.

And the next.

For Tres it was bad. It was bad for all of us, but for him, and I didn't know why, it was real bad.

Ugly bad.

Crazy bad.

We cleaned out those corpses. We made it all nice for CNN and BBC. All that burnt, nasty flesh. All the char and brain and bone. All the screams that got frozen. All those boys like Tres and me who got torched and knew in those awful seconds they really were toast.

When they pulled us back to Kuwait City, there were still wells on fire. It still looked like hell and the air all sticky with stinky smoke, and it was hard to breathe. When we got there, I told Tres I was goin' out to score some booze or hash or whatever I could find and get whacked and asked him to come with me.

And he said no.

He had the funniest, saddest smile.

And when I come back, he'd blown his brains out.

I never figured why my sweet nigger had to kill himself. After what we'd seen and what we'd done.

But I did know then—when I held that bloody head in my lap and made that sound I'd never made before and have never made since, till

Bowman came runnin' and then just started screamin' *"Oh Christ Oh Christ Oh Christ!"*—I knew somewhere really way far deep inside me what I'd be doin' till the day I died. I would keep those children—those boys and the girls—from ever havin' to do what Tres did, what I did, what we did, see what we saw, touch what we touched, have those cinders seep into our skin and make our souls all filthy and dusty, greasy and sad, just to make sure we knew how Hell would be.

So they'd never have to have those ash folk inside.

My first kill was messy. It didn't work right. I had to stab and stab and stab with that goddamn ice pick till he finally dropped. There was blood all over that rest stop and all over me. I had to wash in the sink and use that fucked-up blow-dryer and walk half-naked to my car for the shirt I'd stowed.

And then I drove.

I drove like crazy through Wisconsin and Minnesota and North Dakota and Montana.

And then I settled in for a while in Idaho and figured my mistakes.

The next time, with the whore in Boise, it was clean and fast.

It's been clean and fast ever since.

I mean, Jesus, I'm supposed to be an angel.

Tres told me that one night, that I looked like an angel.

I laughed. "What fuckin' bullshit!"

But he didn't laugh. "No bullshit," he said real quiet. "You look like the angels in the stained glass windows at my church."

"Well, fucker." And I stroked that nappy hair. "'Bout the only angels we'll ever be is the fallen ones. That's us."

And he snickered. I couldn't tell if he meant it. "Guess that's all poor boys can ever be, huh?"

"You got it, dude."

I didn't know then, of course. That it was that night that Tres made
me what I am now. Goin' around, savin' em from what happened to us.
I wish he were here. We'd make a real pair of Angels from Hell.
The both of us with our ashmen from the Highway of Death.
Just two silly, killin' fuckers.

I take a long draw off my traveler and stick him back under the seat.
My throat burns good, and I feel the fire rise outta my stomach and
up my chest and floodin' my brain, just shootin' right past that ice pick
I got in my pocket.
Tres'll be with me soon. From the other side.
He always rides back with me when I'm done.
I'm in New Mexico, I think.
I'm on a mission.

Against the door frame with her glass of wine, she felt a peaceful laziness that passed over her too seldom in the afternoon. It usually came only at night, when the children were in bed, when, from the deck, she could hear but not see the surf tumbling rhythmically below. She squinted in the sunlight, gazing over the rooftops to the distant beach and, beyond it, the shimmering Pacific. For that instant, Lois let herself marvel at her good fortune—having this view, this house. Rare were the specialists in John Ford who could afford it.

Nor could she have but for Eric.

She glanced inside. He was kneeling beside the table, tightening its hinges with a tiny screwdriver. As he rolled the shaft with his fingertips, she admired the tracery of bone and vein on the back of his hand, his sinewed forearm, the biceps that, even at rest, strained the sleeves of his T-shirt.

She smiled.

When they had been married, neither of them had paid much attention to biceps.

He swayed back on his heels and stood. "You now have a functioning gate-leg table, and I rewired that lamp in Amy's room, which should be okay as long as she and her pals don't swing on the cord." He popped the screwdriver into the toolbox and slid it with his foot into the corner. "So, do I get a prize?"

"Try the Zinfandel. Or that Australian Chardonnay is nice. And come on out!" she yelled over her shoulder, moving to one of the chairs beneath the awning in the far corner of the terrace.

He emerged with a beer. "Still early for anything too potent," he explained, sliding into the place across from her. "Say, is that pastel in the hall downstairs yours?"

"No, no. I picked it up at the campus art show last year. I haven't done anything in years."

"Thought you might have started again. You really were pretty good, you know." He raised the can. She noticed blood where he had somehow barked his knuckles. *"Tchin-tchin."*

She made an exaggerated grimace as she toasted him back. *"Merde."*

The afternoon was warm, though the sea breeze put the slightest chill in the air. She settled into the cushions and breathed deep. It made her a little dizzy.

"Did you look at the VCR?"

"Yep." He shook his head. "Some things are just too complicated. You'll have to talk to Rob. I can't figure out what the hell he's done to it."

"Oh, I'll just take it in or get a new one. He certainly doesn't know what's wrong."

"I can look again if you like."

"No. Forget it, Eric. You've done enough." She grinned across the table at him. "'It's so nice to have a man around the house,'" she warbled.

He smiled wistfully. "Don't I know it."

Earlier on, it would have bothered her, back when the children were small and the divorce was a fresh wound. But now, it was easier. They could joke back and forth about it. Eric was hurting anyway, and it made no sense to make it an issue.

"Do you think he'll come by?"

"No," she said gently. "It's a phase, but a longish one."

It had been a year since Rob had seen his father. The break occurred out of the blue when he turned fourteen. He seemed to have adjusted to the notion. Both he and Amy visited Eric in Marin regularly; both of them had liked Mark. And then, from one day to the next, the boy balked and had been balking ever since. He had sent all his fifteenth birthday presents back to the Bay Area unopened. He was spending the weekend with friends.

"I guess you're right. I probably wouldn't have dealt with it very well if it had been my dad when I was his age." He laughed softly. "I really thought times had changed."

"Uh-huh."

When they met, she reflected, times had been changing very quickly indeed, or so it seemed, and her interest in 'Tis Pity She's a Whore and Renaissance iconography vaguely embarrassed her when she sat with Eric and his law school friends as they discussed the Court, the applications of the Voting Rights Act, the defenses for civil disobedience. All her passions seemed musty and more than a little suspect. That was why she had worked so hard on her drawing, producing elaborate, artful posters for the grape boycott and the Anti-C.I.A. Coalition and Students Against Racism. This gave her certain credentials in Eric's circle. It was also how she first got him into bed—by offering to sketch him nude. From pose to a variety of positions had not taken long. In all the time since, she had never found a more inventive lover.

"Have you heard much out of Mark?"

"I ran into him at a fundraiser in The City. He's got a new flame, I guess," he said neutrally, then added, smirking, "a good five years older than me at least."

"That's what you get for staying young."

It was right to be complimentary. She had noticed earlier, when he was checking the fan belts for her, that his severely styled hair was, indeed, beginning to thin, just as he'd told her.

She played with the stem of her goblet. "I know you'd've said something, but there isn't anybody new?"

He took a long suck on his beer. "Nope. Not yet."

"You're being . . . careful?"

He smiled. "Yes, Mommy. Are you?"

It had been nearly a year since she had slept with anyone. The affair with Donald had been uninspiring, and she had called it off with little regret. Aside from a brief flurry right after the divorce, she had never played the field much, and that sporting, she knew now, was largely anger.

"Well? Are you?"

"Oh, Eric." She sighed. "It's been so long, my clitoris is learning shorthand."

"Now, now. A marketable skill. Lots of openings in the service sector." He gestured with his beer can. "But seriously, you can never be sure when opportunity'll knock. Don't go out without your rubbers. I'll leave you some when I go."

She did not entirely like the irony. Her ex-husband checking up, leaving her the condoms that, in another time, another place, he would have tucked into that now estranged son's pocket.

"I don't know, hon. They can always break or come off. It happened to us, remember?" For a week after, she had taken DES or something. She still wondered if that seven days of precaution would give her cancer.

"You're not screwing around too much up there, are you?" she asked tentatively.

"Not much," he offered. "Not at all, really. Screwing, I mean." He took another slug of beer. "I've been getting into S&M."

"S&M!" She made an appalled face. "Eric, that *is* perverse."

"Don't be a prude, Lois," he tut-tutted. "No exchange of body fluids. It's very erotic really, if you take it slow. The pain disappears, and then you just slip into some other space." His voice and eyes had turned dreamy. "Besides, there's something wonderfully subversive about taking rituals of oppression and making them the rituals of love."

She shook her head. That was one of the things that had drawn her to him, of course, that barely restrained extremity. Something Jacobean, Caroline: an excessiveness that could not be bridled and sent him now plunging across new erotic heavens like some aging Icarus.

"You're a crazy man," she said to him. "You always were."

"That's right. 'Still crazy after all these years,'" he crooned. "What time's Amy back?"

"Five-thirty."

"Want to hit the beach?"

It had been forever since she had been. It really was too late in the day. By the time they got there, it would be cold.

She narrowed her eyes against the glare off the distant water.

"Sure," she said.

In the old days, in summer, trapped in the inland smog, they had lived for the beach. It had meant a thirty mile drive in her car, a battle-scarred Pontiac, or his, an endlessly reconditioned VW van, but it seemed a small price for waves, fresh air, a respite from the consuming seriousness of their lives on campus. It was not that they did not party: dance, drink wine, drop acid. But they studied hard and, more than that, approached what was happening in the world in a way she found difficult, now, to explain to her own students. That commitment, that fine and righteous intoxication of belief, so heady and yet such a burden, and ever more so as the 'sixties faded and the 'seventies made them sorrowful, cramped, besieged.

Perhaps it was the weight of that commitment that had enraged her more than anything when Eric took off for the Bay Area with his new law firm and his newly discovered orientation, leaving her behind with kids and car and her thesis half done. They had never really talked about it, and likely he did not become the disco bunny and bathhouse barracuda she imagined during those nights when Amy was still a baby. But, as she wrestled with *Perkin Warbeck* into the wee hours, a picture of him snorting poppers and shimmying under the strobe lights would muscle suddenly into her battle with the text, like one of those caped promoters always interrupting the rigged matches Rob watched worshipfully on Saturday afternoons. Her jaw would clench, and her eyes would mist at the thought of the freewheeling youth she never had.

There before wheeling free was dangerous.

She turned over on her stomach and watched him now, playing at the ocean's edge. He still looked good at forty, having filled out in the years since he had left her. Scrawniness had been the style back then.

The one thing she still could not adjust to was his hair above his ears. She had loved to play with those locks that brushed his shoulders, fell in an aureole like spun sunlight around his head while he slept. For years, she had kept the studies of him she had done in charcoal one summer, until the mildew ruined them. He had gotten shorn after a month in San Francisco.

She always wished she had snipped a ringlet once as a memento.

"Whew!" He raced up out of the waves—glistening, boyish—and *whumped* down beside her, spattering her with cold brine icier for the sun on her skin. She sat up with a jerk.

"Shame on you!"

"Aw, come on, old lady, don't be a gremmie or whatever the hell it was." He stood and pulled her to her feet and then along behind him. "Once more into the beach, dear friends!"

She was laughing so hard when they hit the water, she got a mouthful of foam. As she fell into the surf, she dragged him along with her, and they both went under. They splashed and dunked each other in the waves, breathless from giggles and the chilling sea. In that moment, from a distance, they might have been mistaken for two sweethearts, a man and a woman only just blossomed, teetering on the brink of potential.

Though she was really a bit old for it, before Amy went to bed, Eric read to her. Lois rarely had time for such things, and she resented it a little, much as it warmed her when, on her way from the study to the coffeepot, she heard his sonorous voice lilting through the house. It was a fine mid-range tenor, the amber of dry sack she had imagined once as she listened to him at one of those endless political meetings, explaining yet another time some fine point of strategy. Now, as its gentle timbres wrapped around the archaisms of some fairy tale or other, as she stood in the dark kitchen, she could briefly wish things had worked out, or that it were way back when, in a moment when a little girl and her father together on the sofa would be unremarkable. Was it so much easier before, with people staying together come hell or high water, till death did them part, for the sake of the children? Was that odd serenity she remembered her parents possessing worth envying, or was it merely a kind of shell shock, the mask of desire in shrouds?

After the last Shakespeare essay was marked, she made two gin and tonics and took them to the living room. Eric was hunched over the coffee table, one of the smoke alarms gutted before him. She paused for an instant to watch him as he toyed with the wires and jiggled the battery.

"Be careful. If that thing goes off, Amy'll have a stroke." She sat down across from him and handed him his drink.

"I think it's shot. It's the one from the hall by Rob's room. We can get a new one tomorrow morning on the way to the airport." He pushed the jumble aside. "So, any budding Kittredges in this crop?"

"Afraid not. Just the usual: Macbeth as henpecked husband; Hamlet as indecisive wimp; the unsullied passion of Romeo and Juliet versus the filthy lust of Antony and Cleopatra." She took a swallow from her glass. "Undergraduates are so imperial about sex. If it doesn't happen between sixteen and twenty-five, it's repulsive."

"I recall that stage," Eric said. "Someone told me when I was a sophomore that my German professor was having an affair with a graduate student. I found the idea that Fraulein Barrett had any inclinations in that direction unspeakably twisted."

He settled back on the sofa and put his feet up.

"Rob called while you were in the shower," she said.

"Double-checking my flight time?"

She snorted. "Don't be paranoid. I took it as a good sign. It could have been you who answered the phone."

"I guess." Eric shrugged. "Was I asked after?"

"Indirectly. He wanted to know if the VCR was fixed."

"Little prick," he muttered ruefully and scratched at the scab on his knuckles.

She winced, then concentrated on her glass. It was not a question she ought to ask, but she knew she wanted to, had thought about off and on all day. She was afraid he would read it wrong, that he would take offense, or worse, start to talk to her about disability coverage, the benefits arranged for the kids, his will—all with the notion that the reason she cared was the checks he had sent religiously every month since he had left her.

"Eric." She hated the way her voice sounded. Ponderous. Parental. "Eric, have you had that test?"

Midway through a sip, he stopped, set his drink down. He cocked his head, curious. She knew he understood what she meant.

"No." He put his hands behind his head and stretched. "No. I've thought about it. A lot. I have to act as if it were positive. But I don't have to know." He lowered his eyes to meet hers. "Have you?"

"Have I what?"

"Had the test?"

She leaned forward, snorting in frustration. "Eric. No, no, I haven't. It's you who have to worry."

"For the present."

"Yes. Yes. For the present. I don't mean to make it sound like us versus them. . . ."

"Or you versus me."

Lois slumped. "Eric, don't. I just . . ."

He smiled, kindly, and sat up straight. "I know, Lo. I know."

He lowered his feet, stood, walked to the open screen.

It was a few minutes before she followed him onto the terrace.

He was leaning over the railing, smoking dope.

She slipped alongside him. "Eric, really!" she piped half-seriously. "What would the kids think?"

"I don't know about Amy. Rob would probably be pissed at missing out. Here." He passed her the joint.

Below, the sea pounded anonymous in the distance, infinitely black, the hill leading up to them touched only with the faintest glow of streetlights and televisions. They toked back and forth, unspeaking. The muzziness of marijuana wafted through her, and her body hummed with an old familiar warmth.

Eric puffed rapidly on the roach. It flared bright, suffusing his face in a warm gold.

Then it was dark again.

"The lamps are going out all over loveland," he whispered. "We shall not see them lit again in our lifetime." He rolled the dead cinder in his fingers, then popped it in his mouth. His hand floated away from his face, out before him in a gesture that embraced all the sleeping world below. "Our poor babies."

Her cheeks were wet. A sudden, deep sadness rose through her, through the cozy shimmer of the dope. "Goddamn it, Eric. It's so unfair."

"What?"

She snuffled loudly. "I don't know. Everything. Life. It's no good. Things didn't used to be like this. Shit!" She dabbed her eyes with the back of her hand.

He laid his arm gently on her shoulder and stroked her cheek. "Don't cry, Lo. Don't cry."

"Why did it get so complicated? Everything's too complicated."

There was a sweet, soft pause.

"Oh, I don't know. I think it's always been complicated. It just seems harder when you're living it." He looked out toward the invisible sea. His voice was very soft. "Sammy, Mark's little brother—you met him once—Sammy died about six months ago. He was twenty-four. We took his ashes out on a boat, out near the Golden Gate. Only six of us could make the trip. It was just a little motorboat. The rest of the people at the funeral had to stay on the dock.

"And as we sailed away, I looked back, and I flashed on a story my dad told me once, about when he shipped out during World War II, looking back at the pier where all the parents and wives and lovers and friends were, standing there, waving good-bye. And then they all scattered back across the country in trains and cars and buses, not knowing who on those boats was going to live and who was going to die." His voice vanished thinly in the darkness.

He cleared his throat. "Maybe someday I'll have a chance to tell Robbie that story. And Amy, too. And then, years and years from now, when something else hopelessly unfair happens, they'll remember."

Past midnight, they went inside. He kissed her cheek and headed for the guest room.

"Eric."

He stopped on the third stair and turned.

"Eric. I want you to know, if . . ." But did it need be said after all? "Eric. I . . . I . . ."

She saw him again as that first time, at the demonstration on the steps of the university chancellor's house: serious, vulnerable, unflustered.

Brave.

But the world now was such a different, different place.

"Before you go tomorrow, can I . . . can I sketch you?"

He looked at her quizzically.

"You can keep your clothes on."

He smiled. "Sure," he said.

Then he raised his arm slightly and, though it seemed to take him an instant or two to remember how, he formed two fingers into a V.

"Peace, Lo," he said.

And she said, "Peace."

What It Came To

for Darcy and Dick

The lighter was new. A Zippo. He knew she had noticed when he tried to light her cigarette.

She noticed things like that.

That was why, he supposed, she was a good social worker.

He hadn't wanted to meet her at her office. But it was private on Saturdays, she said.

Besides, she had work to do.

"Is it always this cold?"

"It gets colder."

He leaned his forehead on the window. His breath misted the glass. Even through it, he could feel the wind.

"You like it? Chicago, I mean."

"Yes."

He turned to face her. She played with the locket around her neck. Her hair was dirty, and she was paler than he remembered. She'd lost the tan she'd had when they met in Acapulco.

He looked outside.

"When did you find out?"

"I missed my second period. Then I went to the doctor."

"That was . . .?"

"The day I called. A week ago Thursday."

He sighed. "I'm sorry. I got tied up. The firm, and this thing with my dad . . ."

"Your father's been dead six months."

"The will's a mess. I'm sorry," he added meaninglessly.

"Don't be. L.A.'s a long way from Chicago, much less Acapulco."

"Cut it out."

"Some little social worker from Chicago. Who'd've thought?"

"Shut up."

"Shut up yourself."

In the silence, he could hear the wind. Always the wind, ever since he arrived, bitter off the lake. The lake was gray and the sky was gray and the city was gray and there was the wind—gouging the streets.

"I should have come sooner."

"Yes. You should've."

He had convinced himself it was decent to come at all. It was hard being new at the firm, and the problems with the estate made him crazy. It had been just a five-day fling in Mexico to celebrate passing the bar and getting the job, a celebration deferred by the funeral. If things got said or promises made there on the beach—well, that was part of the game.

If this hadn't happened, it would have died a natural death.

Even so, he could just have sent a check.

But that wouldn't have been facing up.

His father always said facing up was important.

He snorted a single, mirthless laugh.

"What?"

"We were careful."

"Oh, Jesus."

He flared momentarily. "We were!"

"But not careful . . . enough."

"I guess not."

The walls were green, like in an operating room. He had read somewhere that, that way, you couldn't see the blood.

"What are we going to do?" he said.

"Want to marry me?"

"No."

"Then there's the other way."

The radiator clanked and clattered. She had had to deal with it every day, he thought. That's what social workers do, after all—help the poor and the hungry and the knocked up.

He cleared his throat.

"You're sure it's mine."

Her hand went white on the locket. Then she stood and came quickly toward him, almost at a canter. She cracked her palm flat across his cheek.

"I hate you!" she hissed.

The sting spread across his face. He took a very deep breath. "Me, too, I guess," he said softly.

"It's got to get done." She began to pace, arms tight across her breasts. "Soon."

"It's the second month?"

"At least."

"You know where you can get it?"

"Yes."

"They won't screw it up?"

She flashed a tight smile. "They know how."

"How much?"

She told him.

"I'll give it to you. In cash."

"I want half."

"No. I'll pay."

"I want half," she repeated, deliberately.

He felt a little sick, like at the funeral.

He handed her the money. "Here."

And his father said *Flesh of my flesh.*

"Good."

Blood of my blood.

"I'm going for a walk," he said.

And the Father said *Earth to earth.*

"Fine."

Ashes to ashes.

At the door, he stopped, turned toward her, feeling the knowledge on his face.

"That's our kid."

She looked at him with something like pity. "Yes."

Dust to dust.

The stairs were linoleum. They were drab and scuffed and beginning to warp. He took them two at a time.

Outside, it was hard and dark. The clouds scudded overhead, and the wind slashed off the lake, crying between the buildings, raising swirls of grime and garbage.

It knifed into him.

"Goddamn."

He wiped his eyes.

He had none of his boxer brother's grace, nor his father's swagger that she remembered as the first thing she had noticed there at the mixer at the Knights of Columbus Hall. Perhaps he did lumber, as his brother said, but Joseph was always putting the worst face on things. No, she thought, watching him from the kitchen window as he came out of the garage, his was a solid step, not a loutish one. It had an earnestness to it like Petie himself, the kind of thing that, had he been her brother instead of her son, would have been expected in those destined for the Church.

They had planned a bigger family, she and Bill, but after Petie was born, the pregnancies just didn't go right. After she lost the twins, they had decided, despite Father Conner's injunction, that the two boys were all God intended. She had gone to her sister Margaret's in Pawtucket to have the ligation and had suffered pangs of conscience for years every time she took communion. It was only after Father Weggett replaced Father Conner at St. Catherine's that she felt she could confess what she had done, and he, who was young and handsome and sometimes used folk songs during Mass, had told her the Church's attitudes were changing and that probably the penance of her conscience those last five years had been penance enough.

Petie lifted another box off the driveway and wrestled it into the Gomes boy's truck. She still did not like his moving out. And she surely did not like the Gomes boy. Home was still good enough for Joseph, who was almost twenty-six and over four years on the police force. She could still not understand why both he and her husband, when Petie announced his plan, had sided with him and not with her.

At first, at the dinner table, she was simply stunned. Children— boys or girls, it didn't matter—moved out of the house when they got married, period, despite what was happening all over the country, had been happening really for years now. But the Irish were different that way. For Irish, family meant something. Besides, everybody knew young people away from home were always inviting trouble to walk right through the door.

"Petie," she had said, "what a silly idea. Why would you want to do that?"

"Ma," he said. "I'm almost twenty-three. I need to learn to get along on my own. And David'll have to give up his place if he can't find somebody to share it."

"Well," she said testily, "David's problems are no concern of yours."

She had distrusted the Gomes boy from the first time she laid eyes on him eight months before. He and Petie had met at the pool at the Y. He had taught Petie to play paddleball, and now they were lifting weights together. As time went on, Petie spent more and more time with him. He was a big, dark kid, not tall but stocky, Portuguese— half-Azorean really—who, she didn't doubt, had some colored blood back there somewhere. He was two years out of the army, worked in the New Haven yards, and had a hard time holding a conversation with her because every third word out of his mouth was dirt. He censored himself when he talked to her, but she had caught enough of what he said when he didn't realize she was listening to know the type.

She couldn't understand why Petie liked him—Petie, thoughtful and polite. If it were Joseph who had brought the Gomes boy home, she might not have been so surprised. He had taken up with all kinds, which is what had made him perfect for police work. But Petie was always gentler. He was the one who had been to college—a real college, not some trade school. He would have made a good priest, she had no doubt: devout, concerned, hardworking, and sympathetic. She had suggested it a couple times, but he would have none of it. He did his job at the bank and dreamt of being an illustrator—writing children's books for which he would do the drawings himself. She wished sometimes she knew somebody who knew somebody on Beacon Hill who would help him get a start.

"Doesn't sound like such a bad idea," Joseph had said that night. "If Petie wants to move out, let him. More roast beef for me." He smirked, passing his plate down the table for his father to shovel on another helping.

Joseph was always contrary, not at all what people said the eldest son was supposed to be. He had always belonged to his father.

She thought he was merely being difficult. "Joc . . ."—which he had insisted recently was the proper way to address him, not Joseph or Joey—"you are the limit!" She stared down the table at her husband. "Bill, why don't you say something?"

Her husband looked up tiredly. She knew he hated to intervene. He had been a listless father, something she could say only because she loved him. If the boys had been girls, it might have been different, but with Joseph and Peter, he had been mostly a disciplinarian and nothing more. In the end, Joey had spent his life trying to please him, and maybe, just maybe, he'd had some success. But Petie had never really even made the effort. From the time he was in diapers he'd somehow read the realities of the situation and so never cared too much what his father had to say.

"If Petie wants to move out, let him." Bill shrugged. "David's a nice enough kid. What do you want, Eleanor? It's time he spent some time with men his own age."

That stung her, for that had always been one of Bill's complaints, that Petie spent too much time with girls.

"Why the hell can't he hang out with the boys on the corner like his brother used to?" Bill grumbled while Petie was still in high school. "Cripes, at least once in a while."

Eleanor had let out a sniff of surprised outrage. The fights and the shouting and the strappings from back then, when Bill was convinced that Joey had fallen in with the wrong crowd and was sure to end up in jail before he even got his diploma! The swearing and the hitting had made her physically sick.

"He'll get himself a one-way ticket to the slammer," Bill had thundered, "and I won't lift a finger to help him! Not a goddamn finger! And whatever happens to him in there happens, and it won't be pretty! He asked for it, the little bastard!"

How he had hit him.

The irony that Joseph had ended up in police work was not lost on her.

"Well," she said briskly, "we can talk later, Petie. Let's not ruin our dinner."

She got up to bring the pie she had baked that afternoon.

○ ○ ○

Petie had kept his own counsel for the next several days. She was certain his father and brother had not noticed, but she had, as she had
noticed for the last two or three years that he had seemed ever quieter,
ever less communicative than he had been when he was a boy. In high
school, it seemed he couldn't wait to give her the rundown of his day
from start to finish, although she was trying to vacuum or cook or
get the outgrown clothes and worn-out appliances ready for the rum-
mage sale at St. Catherine's. He would tumble through the door, bub-
bling with news about the yearbook staff and the drama club, about his
American history class and the choir. He was a good student and had
found his niche in a smorgasbord of activities that she took great pride
in, even if his father didn't.

School had not been the easiest row to hoe for him, especially after
sixth grade or so. It wasn't his studies or his teachers, but his class-
mates. Though he was big, he was often bullied by the other boys, who
called him names and even punched him around a couple of times.
The neighborhood did not take kindly to those with higher aspirations, that she knew. Joseph, in that sense, was the true product of his
world—a brawler and a marginal student, a boy who started smoking
when he was eleven. He had even had a few tangles with the law—
nothing serious, but enough to give him a scare when he applied for the
police academy. Her sister's sons idolized him growing up; at the same
time, they wanted nothing to do with Petie, though Margaret herself
said outright she thought Joey was mean and a bad influence on her
Tommy and Mike and Freddy.

Despite her maternal instincts, Eleanor had not even challenged
her, for, in those years, even she found her elder a little scary, and, in
the years since, she thanked God every night on her knees that he had

ended up as a man in blue rather than as a bookie or a car thief or one of the enforcers for the Bulgers.

Joe himself had had little sympathy for his little brother back then. Indeed, he had called him names with all the rest. She had given him a good slap for it once, when he turned on Petie, who was only twelve and had started to cry when some of the boys were playing catch and he skinned his elbow when he had dived for the ball—probably just to impress them—and fallen on the asphalt of the driveway.

"Ah, shut up, you little fruit!" Joey had mocked as he stood there with his arms crossed.

She had gotten up from the stoop where she was transplanting geraniums to put out in front, walked across the scrap of yard behind their three-decker, pulled her arm back as far as she could, and smacked her high school sophomore son squarely across the cheek.

"Don't you ever, ever speak to your brother that way again!" she snarled with a fury that frightened even her.

The red left by her palm was flecked with potting soil there on his skin.

Joey had turned sixteen and was twice her size by then, and he had to have been humiliated in front of all his friends.

But after a flare of shock and anger crossed his eyes, he had simply turned away.

"Ah, Ma . . ." he had whined and left it at that.

It was easier to read him than it was to read Petie these days.

He had grown away from her. Something had happened at college—of that she was sure—though he had come home on the T every night. He had had a scholarship to B.C. The Jesuits had done right by him, and she was endlessly proud in the neighborhood: through the honor role and the A's he had earned and the way the brothers she occasionally met (along with the odd women they insisted on taking on as instructors at what had always been a good college for Catholic boys) said that Petie was outstanding—a real scholar, someone who would make a mark, go beyond his roots, outstrip his father and his brother. Petie was special, and he would represent something that was beyond the entire consciousness of three-decker lives, regardless of what it took.

She heard them outside. Petie and the Gomes boy.

There was a loud *smack*!

Eleanor caught it, just out of the corner of her eye as she had slipped past the kitchen window.

He had hit him. He had hit him hard! Right across the behind! The two of them were on the driveway.

And Petie laughed.

He laughed when David Gomes hit him there in the driveway. He had struck him with one of the paddleball paddles that they used when they were sweating in that world of the Y that was, for Eleanor, entirely foreign, and she heard the Gomes boy say: "You little fuck, I will make your ass pay!"

And Petie laughed. He had laughed. As she looked out the window half-hidden by the sheers, there in the kitchen beside the breakfast dishes in the drainer, she saw him grab at the Azorean's crotch and giggle like a child.

"Watch it!" the Gomes boy hissed, glancing around. In that feral scan—up and down, back and forth—did he see her there behind the nylon made to look like lace?

Petie giggled again.

Eleanor stepped back from the window as if suddenly it were an open oven door and the heat singed her eyebrows. Her hand went to her lips. This was the boy she had hoped would have understood what she wanted. This was the boy that she had hoped might give her what she had always sought in Bill. What she could never hope for from Joseph.

Someone finer. Someone who could understand the aspirations she had to go sometimes to the symphony there on Huntington Avenue, the art museum on the Fenway. A man like she sometimes saw on television, like the priests at Boston College, like the Kennedys, who had left behind their shanty Irish roots and talked about paintings and books and operas.

But in that instant, she realized Petie belonged to the Gomes boy. That there was something primal and terrible drawing her good Irish son to that dark Azorean ex-soldier, something perhaps her husband and her elder son had seen and oddly understood, which made them want to send Petie into exile—away from them, away from her.

That night, she made dinner for them all—Petie's farewell dinner at home. Joe and David traded stories about boxing, and even Bill, never much for table talk, got drawn into the conversation, offering his comments on his minimal hand-to-hand training in the service. Petie spent most of the meal silent, his soft smile bespeaking a strange satisfaction, as if—for the first time in his life, even at one remove—he had entered that hard world inhabited by his father and his brother.

Eleanor sat at her end of the table in a daze of isolation, the foundations of all she thought she knew creaking beneath her, the child she thought she knew suddenly foreign and inscrutable. She said nothing though and, deep in her heart, she knew she never would. She felt the same panic she had felt long ago, once when the boys were little, on the beach on Cape Cod. Joey had towed Petie out on an air mattress, far into the calm waters of the bay. The sound of little boys' laughter had drifted over the water, and she had been seized there beside the gentle surf with a momentary certainty that Petie would fall off the raft and drown, and neither Bill nor she nor Joey would be able to save him.

That night, as they got ready for bed, Bill was oddly expansive. "Seems like a great kid. Real street smarts. He'll be good for Petie. Joe thinks so."

She would never tell him, of course. Not Bill, not Joe. Not her sister, Margaret. She could not tell even Father Weggett, she thought, what she had heard that afternoon—she against the wall beside the kitchen window.

David's words had come out in a husky whisper. "You know I love you, you little faggot."

And then there was Petie's breathless voice, blooming with a wanting she knew she could never comprehend. "Yes, David. Yes. I love you, David. I love you, too."

Swim

10 September 1950 / for Joey Houser

Swim, your father whispered. Swim as far as you can go.

Beside the lake, your clothes piled on the shore you'd always known.

Ste. Claire, her pitchy lapping tickling your feet, above, a star-sown peace of velvet night.

Now swim! your father said.

You'd had a dream.

The hair on your arms and legs rose up against a chilly breeze sprung from the west. White-girdled with the rest of you nut-brown, a summer's worth of sunlight-dappled skin. That day, with all the rest, you'd searched the yards, the woods, the beach. . . .

And then you had a dream.

There was a neighbor boy of eight or nine, a few years younger than you were, you—brawny high school lineman. And one fine day, he vanished into air, so through the dark and into the next day, you sought the boy with everybody else.

Before you had that dream.

They'd found him dead, but worse than that small, shattered skull were all those other things that had been done. How much the child had suffered till that rock had crushed his brain.

And then you had your dream.

You heard the teasing, goading, felt the lurch from fun to fear as that small boy was changed into a squirrel, a bird, a bug. A huge snake loomed above him.

Then the knife, and then those other things . . .

I've had this dream.

He looked at you with loathing, wonder, shame. This was a man who'd been to war. And now his son, his boy, revealed himself to be a demon sprung from his own seed.

He turned away and retched when you told him of your dream.

When he turned back, his eyes were wet. Come on, he croaked. And with him through the night you wound to Lake Ste. Claire, a walk you'd made a thousand times, but this time strangely different, as if all the world had changed.

As if you saw it in a dream.

Take off your clothes, he hissed then on the shore, and so you did, your head abuzz as if with beer, as light as dew. You stood there now before him, limber-limbed, as naked as he first beheld you, but you could tell he saw you not at all.

Because you had that dream.

Swim . . . , he said, the word as soft as breath.

And something told you that your hapless father hoped you'd drown. Your body never found, there'd be no horror, family stain, as if your disappearing meant that deeds had not been done and that you never had that dream.

. . . far as you can.

You knew it had been you. Your father knew that, too. There was no time now for a second chance.

You looked across the gentle, still expanse and heard it call you in a voice pitched high, that of a little boy of eight or nine.

You dreamt.
You swam.

There at the gully.

That summer. There's where it happened.

Me and Roy.

Funny how we ended up again in my truck, the bottle open.

"What the fuck were you thinking?" He laughed. "Jeez, you were a sad little fuck."

And he laughed again and took a draw off the Jim Beam.

We were arguing about a song. Well, not arguing, but I was telling him that, for years, I thought the words said one thing when, according to him, they said something completely different. I guess it made me look stupid.

But to see Roy laugh like that. That was worth it.

Guys make assholes of themselves for their friends. They will do the dumbest shit so their buds can break up and break down—even if it hurts or there's blood or something. And I just couldn't believe Roy was back and that we were at the gully, and we were sucking down the Beam again at three o'clock in the morning.

Roy and me, we played baseball. He was shortstop, and I played second base. Those two men on the field have one soul. They have to know not just each other's heads but each other's bodies—the moves and muscles and the nerves, what he's sure about and what he doesn't quite know.

We were a song. People really said that. On a double play, he could slam me an underhand fireball I could grab right in the fartherest craw of my mitt and tag that boy out, out, and out again, then fire it on to first if I had to. No ump hassles those times, believe me.

And he'd grin. And I'd grin. And we'd know we'd done a good job.

Roy went to college.

I wasn't smart that way.

That's no big deal. I wasn't like a lot of the guys I ran with. I knew they'd go away. And I knew that those wimps on the debate team in my civics class would probably be my bosses in twenty years. I knew what my dad had gone through, and my uncles, and I'd listened to them talk.

Roy wasn't like me. He wasn't just a hotshot high school shortstop. He got mostly A's and B's, even in stuff like chemistry and American history. We had a couple of classes together, and he'd let me crib off his tests, and he even wrote an English paper for me once when it looked like I was going to get a D. Would my old man have whaled my ass for that one! I think the teacher, Mrs. Krebbs, knew I couldn't have written that paper, but she gave me a B anyway.

So you can see, there was no one special to me like Roy. That was true from the very first. We used to go out, just us two, and get drunk after the games. I would look at him out there in the pine grove after a game when we were fifteen, Bud in hand, and feel something. I never felt it when I looked at Billy Prowthrow or Tommy Evans. I didn't know why.

He went to college.

I went to construction.

That is what my family does.

We are carpenters. We build things. We go into a house and look at the damage the goddamn plumbers have done slamming around looking for the busted pipes. We look at the design for a deck some dude wants to pay three thousand dollars for that will cost eight thousand dollars, and that's not including labor. Guys who work in offices never really understand what it takes to set that beam just so, how your arm can throb after pounding two inch nails all day, how things can go bad wrong with a circular saw if you're not paying attention, how you can use bread to bleed out pipes when you've gotta solder. They think you've got shit for brains and just want to rip them off.

But I'm honest in what I do. My dad and my uncles taught me that.

I look at the world like they did. There is an empty space, but I see a house there. Or a wall. Or a closet. A screened porch. A rec room. A workshop . . .

I do a good job.

o o o

It was Alma Bristol's idea, and we had never done it before. It had to do with the Internet, that all of a sudden she could contact absolutely everybody we had gone to high school with. And we, from this little buttfuck town in the middle of nowhere, were going to have a reunion.

Twenty-five years? I looked at the invite on the dining table, bone-tired, with Cindy at the stove and Jason and Linda and Ashley all ripping and racing and yammering at once, and thought, "What the hell?"

Did I really want to see Alma (who had moved to Portland, Oregon) or MadBlast Thomas or Beverley the Beverley or Glenn, the quarterback who knocked up the head cheerleader, Connie, and then, good Catholics like they were, got married? What kind of TV show did that come off of?

But then I thought of Roy. And of course I was going.

I did think the whole idea was silly, and I told people so. Out on the site, some kid almost young enough to be one of mine said, "Hey, I hear you dudes are having a reunion."

It was that weird. In this town, nobody ever re-yuned. You got the hell out or you didn't. If you did, you made sure you didn't come back, and if you didn't, you didn't like to be reminded of it.

And I said, "Yep. Well, it was Alma Bristol's idea, and I reckon we were all dumb enough to let her get to us. Now you get those fuckin' posts up before I can your ass!"

o o o

Roy went to State. He didn't play baseball there. He told me the guys who did made us look like a bunch of pansies, that they could throw and bat and steal like pros. I did some pickup games in those days, but I was trying to make journeyman, and, a lot of the time when I was an apprentice, I didn't have the strength, even that young, to do anything but drink a beer in front of the TV and eat takeout from the Peking Palace when I got home from work. It didn't make any difference that my dad and my uncles were in the union. You still had to prove yourself, and they would work a newbie from six until three or four even though you could hardly do anything but drop, knowing you'd be back next morning.

Her name was Allison. I met her once, just for a minute, when she was with him, and they passed through town and were going up north. She was real pretty. And Roy was stupid over her. She came from some ritzy place outside of Philadelphia. She had nice tits and a nice ass, but most of all she had a face like something off the cover of a magazine. I thought then that maybe Roy might be a little too small town for her, but I didn't say anything.

It was just that he was a shortstop.

And Allison looked like she didn't do anybody but pitchers.

So there was that one summer.

Roy had been at school for three years. He was home for vacation, and, on June thirteenth, he got the Dear John. I got the notion later this wasn't a total surprise, that Allison had been checking out some older guy who was going to make a lot of money—not a professor but some guy who was in business or something—and my boy Roy didn't have a Chinaman's chance.

But Roy was twenty.

And it broke his heart.

It's kinda funny, because, even though I felt bad for him, I wondered a little how he couldn't see it coming, or if he didn't, how he could let it run him over like that. I guess I come from people who expect to get run over. We can spot the Allisons a mile away.

So we were in the truck, and he was talking, and we were slamming the Beam, and all of a sudden he started to cry—out of the blue just bawling like some five-year-old because he was so sad that Allison was gone, and it was a bench seat and I just reached over and I hugged him.

And he just cried harder.

He had his head against me, and his body was jerking all over, and I could feel hopelessness just sweating out of him. I had known Roy all my life. Since I was old enough to know anybody. There on the diamond, it was like we'd been one person. I held him tighter, and he was like bawling and bawling, "What am I gonna do? What am I gonna do?"

So I blew him.

I know that'll make you laugh.

Makes me laugh now when I think of it, I guess.

But what was I gonna do? I was a kid, too, and all I knew was that Roy was hurting, hurting really bad. I didn't even think. I kissed him. Not on the mouth. And then I just went down on him. I had never done that before, I swear. But I opened his jeans and put his dick in my mouth and I sucked him. I should have been scared, I guess, or freaked out or something. But what I knew was my buddy was crying. My baseball buddy who was going to do something besides get stuck in our buttfuck town where I was stuck, and this bitch had made him feel so bad, and I had to do something to make him feel better again.

Roy and me played that whole summer. We'd drive to the gully in my truck, and we'd trade the Beam, and then we'd do what we did. Guys will tell you, if they tell you at all, that it only happened once. But if they tell you, it means it happened more than once or that they wanted it to.

Everybody is always shitfaced.

Roy remembered nothing.

I remembered everything.

I won't tell you everything we did. I'm not being proud or stupid. Sure, these days people like to hear all about it. Not just queers, but everybody who reads about this kind of thing standing in line down at the

Kroger at nine p.m. and then talking about it the next day over an Egg McMuffin. Everybody who did it once or twice or again and again. Everybody who, when their buddy hurt, did something they might not have and would never admit it to anybody.

So we're at the gully after the reunion, and we're sucking the Beam, and Roy says: "'Always on time.' That's what the song says. 'Always on time!'":

We are in our forties now. Both of us have been married for more than twenty years. Jason is seventeen, Linda is fourteen, Ashley is nine. Roy's Patty just graduated, and Ronnie is on the JV football squad. Little Pete was an accident; he's only two.

We are not the shortstop and the second baseman we were. Roy's grown a belly. My fingers ache something fierce from all the nails I've hammered, and I'm always taking Motrin. We are not the broken-hearted boy and his buddy we were years ago. This night, there is only some strange echo of a song.

o o o

After that one summer, Roy never came home again. His old man died in late July, and his mom moved down to Florida. He was the young-est, and his brothers and one sister were already long gone. I had not laid eyes on him since that Labor Day weekend, with him heading out to State the next day. We did what we had been doing all that sum-mer—shortstop and second baseman, pitcher and catcher, sealed away from the world by want and shame and Beam.

And now I say: "I know that's right, Roy, but what I always heard was 'Hold the line/ Love is, as always, unkind.'"

Roy laughs. That older face splits in that wide-open grin, and I can see again the boy who could just not understand being loved as he was loved.

"What bullshit!" he hooted.

I nodded.

He was right about the words.

So was I.

Standing by the sink at the window, Gogan could see the truck winding the last mile over the plain. It came slowly, raising little dust, finally gathering speed to make the hill. Watching it, so lonely and small in the bright spring morning, it was odd to think that beyond the next rise and the groves of the next shallow valley was the freeway and, a mile farther, the tattered edges of the city. One day, Gogan knew as he stood there, rinsing his breakfast dishes, his uncle's truck would appear in the distance, and then behind it there would be a house, then another and another. His uncle would rev the motor and fly down the curving road, but the houses would tumble after him, and the truck would disappear behind a laundromat and a Taco Bell. The wave would roll up the hill unspent, crash past the trailer, knock Gogan to the ground. . . .

And when he stood again, in all directions there would be nothing but houses and people and stores. There would be no mustard blooming nor roadrunners, no poppies or coyotes, and the sun would shine pink from smog.

Wiping his hands as he stepped outdoors, Gogan heard the engine on the grade. He squinted in the sunlight. His head ached. The night before had lasted too late, with Toby and Willis there to play cards.

The truck pulled up, and his uncle clambered out. In the back was a bale of barbed wire and a bundle of fence posts.

Gogan nodded. "Where's the break?"

"Big one 'bout halfway to Toby's." His uncle scuffed the gravel. "'nother where lightning struck Tuesday and down by the pond. Lookee here." He reached into the cab, past the gun rack, and pulled out a mud-caked shirt. "We got hippies again."

Gogan laughed. "How many times I got to tell you? Ain't no such thing as hippies no more."

"Hippies. Punks. Assholes. I don't know what you call 'em. Little turds get so socked smokin' or snortin' or whatever they do, they can't even put their goddamn clothes on. One of these days, Gogan, I'm gonna get me one of 'em." He walked to the incinerator and shoved the shirt inside. "All the trash from the house out?"

He lit the papers in a half-dozen places, stepping back as the pile flared. The muddy shirt melted in the flames.

"Go get the hatchet and a couple hammers. We gotta get fencin'."

Gogan opened the screen.

"Hey, Gogan . . ." His uncle's words turned him around to face the smile. "How you feelin'?"

"Not bad, Uncle Buck." Gogan grinned despite the hangover. "Not bad at all."

o o o

Buck McMurtry stood six-foot three in his stocking feet and spoke with something between a twang and a drawl. He came from Oklahoma. His father was a purebred hillbilly out of West Virginia; his mother, a homesick Cajun. From him, Buck inherited a taste for liquor, a difficulty with words, an abiding belief in violence, and a Pentacostal faith made of equal parts ecstasy and shame. To the tiny, wide-eyed woman who had borne him, he claimed he owed only one thing: his real name, Antoine, which only three or four people knew to call him by the time he reached eighteen.

He left home one Christmas after an ugly row with his father, thumbing down 66 with two shirts and an extra pair of jeans, all the way to California. A stint at city life left him lonely and more than a little scared, so he drifted—sometime ditchdigger, orange-picker, roughneck, and cowboy—until he found a job as a ranch hand and caretaker for the Merritt family. They hired him, assigned him, and forgot him, as over the years their interests moved from cattle and goats and horses to the contracts and board meetings that gradually transformed much of the ranch to cash, to subdivisions and shopping centers, and then to bonds and stocks and commodity futures.

After his wife left him, for reasons he never discussed, Buck lived alone. Then he received a letter from Dallas, from a sister who asked that he take her child of a love now also dead, and so Gogan on Greyhound came to live with his Uncle Buck.

At first, it was hard, for the boy—though young—was citywise, and the gruff man and the solitude seemed to drive him half-mad, while Buck hated him both for breaking and recalling his loneliness.

But, with time, their suspicion changed to a bond profound as their usual silence. It did not come suddenly, but rather in the way two solitary animals, unaccustomed to company, gradually learn to live together and finally to care for and groom each another. At first, Buck explained his feelings as no more than a recognition of the usefulness of a second pair of hands, while, for Gogan, the adjustment to his new home seemed simply a matter of survival. But he knew after only a few months that the city, for him, had become as foreign and hateful a place as it was for Buck. The two made a spare and unspeaking life there in the trailer, its quiet broken only by the occasional visits of Toby and Willis and the others who worked the ranch.

When, at sixteen, Gogan left school, he showed no desire to move on. And Buck made no objection, having taught his nephew what he knew about fences and cattle and the weather; how to hunt rabbits, skin possums and even snakes; play poker; fix a busted pump. The boy's remaining, he told himself, was fair return for all he had invested, though secretly he knew that, by now, he had come to depend on Gogan like he had not depended on anyone for many years.

That led, perhaps, to one night, deeply drunk, when Buck told the boy what Gogan thought must be his most terrible secret—that his name was really Antoine. And Gogan, matching confession for confession, revealed he had never known his father, that he truly was a bastard. And then he felt like they were joined like Indians, like blood brothers in the movies. Because of that, he never uttered that soft, French name, and—in the same spirit, he was sure—Buck never mentioned his daddy.

o o o

Though it was early afternoon by the time they reached the pond, they could still see footprints in the mud. The oaks, thick-trunked and wide, spread a shade so deep that, even on the hottest day of summer, when the air was still and heavy, the earth of the grove was moist as spring.

Gogan stood in the truck bed while his uncle studied the break.

The posts were solid, but the wire was badly rusted. Buck swore as he fingered the dull barbs.

"Coil me off forty feet, Gogan, and bring the nails."

"You got snippers?"

"Yeah. Gimme a hand here."

They worked silently, dappled in shade, the leaves and earth soaking up the hammers' echoes.

The job did not take long.

Buck tossed the tools into the pickup, then walked over to a log by the pond and sat down. Gogan followed and squatted beside him.

"Looka that, Gogan. Just look." Buck dug his boot into the dirt and uncovered a crushed beer can. "Little fuckers can't even clean up after themselves." He hawked and spat. "Shit, prob'ly can't even wipe themselves."

Gogan picked up a twig, snapping it idly into smaller and smaller pieces.

"Toby seen 'em," Buck said suddenly, softly. "Just last week. He's on his way to buy beer and he seen 'em. He'da stopped, but he's in a hurry."

"How many?"

"Half a dozen. Maybe nine or ten. Hard to tell in the dark, Toby says. Bunch of skinny-ass guys and their skinny-ass girlfriends come down here to swim naked and smoke that shit and fuck. Bet in a night, one of them girls takes three, four, the whole damn bunch. Little whores. Whores and queers."

"Don't sound queer to me."

Buck snorted and pushed Gogan off balance so he plopped in the mud.

"Hell. They ain't got morals, Gogan. If she gets tuckered out, they just fuck each other."

"Yeah, I guess." He brushed the seat of his pants. "We better get on, huh?"

Buck picked up the beer can and a fallen branch. He tossed the can in the air and smashed it into the water with a loud smack. "Whores and queers."

"You ought to catch 'em," Gogan said. "Get the sheriff or somethin'."

Buck laughed as they headed toward the truck. "Naw. If I was to catch them, I wouldn't want no sheriff around. I want to see 'em squirm good. Blast some salt up their asses or put some juice in the fence. Wait'll they's climbin' over and turn it on."

His voice faded as if he were talking to no one.

Throwing the gear into the truck bed, he looked back once, twice at the fence. Buck could hear them—shouts and warnings and shrieked surprise—and the noise was sweet.

Gogan latched the tailgate and climbed into the cab. "Don't you go gettin' no ideas!" He smiled.

"Huh?" Buck's tone was sharp, like a dreamer's roused in a dark room.

Gogan's smile fell. A sudden, brief disquiet fluttered through him. He faced front.

"Toby comin' up tonight?"

Buck slammed off the brake. "Hell if I know."

o o o

Toby swayed back and forth, foot to foot like a bad boy at school. A hard, bowlegged stump of a man, it looked like he was facing a whupping or worse, his mouth tense, his voice aquiver.

He had not meant to be first with the bad news.

"I'da thought they'da told you. I's sure they would, with the trailer out here and all. I thought you'da known."

Gogan, with the six-pack, stopped midway between Toby and Buck. Only his eyes turned to where his uncle sat, Buck's face bunched tighter and tighter as his head sank toward his chest and his hands clenched fierce at the armrests.

He looked like a man just struck.

"Sold it!" he breathed finally, half-strangled. "Sold it! Goddamn. Goddamn Jew bloodsucker . . . !"

Gogan shook, afraid one or both of them might cry, and Toby, too, for having told and being sad to do it. He watched Buck stand, face the wall, look up, hands on his hips. "You're sure, Toby?" Buck's voice was willed steady. "'Cause if you lie to me I'll kick your ass till . . ."

"I . . . I . . ." There was no escaping. "I'm sure," Toby said slowly. "Evaline told me, up at the house. She's cleanin' up after the party."

"How'd she know?"

"The party, goddamn it!" Toby snapped bravely. "When she went to pick up, the plans is on the table. All the land boys is there, and the lawyers and Merritt and the old lady. . . ."

"Goddamn her! She and her boats and her Hollywood faggots. What the hell's a couple acres, couple thousand acres? Damn bitch in heat. Damn her! Damn the whole damn bunch!"

His hands flew around him like spooked birds, and the veins throbbed in his temples. He brought his palm down flat on the card table, set for the evening's game. The legs wobbled, then splayed as the cards flew up in a jumble. He pushed it over, stood sweaty, half-pleased, as if the table were Mrs. Merritt and her husband and the whole empire of contracts and land deals.

"Just what . . . !" Buck's voice quavered as he tried not to shout. "Just what're they gonna do with all this? You tell me!"

"I dunno. The usual stuff . . ."

"Evaline seen the plans, you said. If she seen the plans, then she told you!"

"The usual stuff!" Toby took a step back. "Houses and a mall up at the north end and a park there at the oak grove and—"

"Hell, yeah!" Buck laughed once like a pistol shot. "Yeah. Can't let them hippies lose that swimmin' hole. Hell! Send the old gal down there for a goddamn gangbang! Christ!" He wheeled. "Gogan! Get that whiskey we bought the other night."

Gogan reached his hand out, his voice low. "Uncle Buck."

"Don't you back talk me, boy!" Buck's eyes narrowed in fury. "You back talk me. I'll kick that city ass of yours halfway to Dallas. Now move!"

He thought for an instant of not obeying, of that word they rarely uttered except in contempt.

They stood, eyes locked, Buck's finger extended in warning.

Gogan turned.

"Good boy!" Buck barked. "You do like you're told; you'll do just fine." He raised the table with one hand. "Bring me a shotglass, too, and a beer mug."

Gogan put the bottle on the table, then the scarred glass mug and the little jar that chipped beef came in.

"That's it. Hand me one of them beers."

Gogan lobbed the can to him softly.

"Now," Buck said, "now here's a trick a fella taught me a long time ago. Get over here, Toby!" Toby followed his finger, eyes down. "He's some slick navy guy from New York or New Orleans or Dallas or somethin'. You, too, Gogan!" He pointed, and Gogan moved. "Probably somebody's daddy." His face was alight with anger. "He showed me this drink, see, and, since he was a sailor and all, he called it a 'depth charge.' What you do is fill up a mug of beer, like so." He popped the can open and poured. "And then you fill the shotglass with whatever shit you got handy and drop it down inside. Real easy. Just slip it right in. And then . . ." He toasted the air and drank in long, deep swallows, thumped the mug on the table, belched. "You just chug it right down. Gimme the rest of the six-pack, Gogan."

Buck fixed another depth charge and pushed it toward Toby.

"Here's to Old Lady Merritt and the development boy who's fuckin' her now," he growled.

Toby took the mug and emptied it without a breath.

Buck made a third drink and passed it to Gogan.

"All right, city boy."

Gogan snatched it away. The beer foamed down; then came the sharp medicine taste of the whiskey. He caught his breath, forced the swallow, and finished it.

Buck turned to Toby. "How's 'bout a refill?"

Toby smiled uneasily. "Naw. Naw, Buck. Maybe we . . ."

"Don't woman out on me." Buck opened a fourth beer and poured the whiskey. "Here's to Evaline and whatever you got offa her all these years."

Toby gave Buck a mean look but drank. Buck made another for himself, then for Gogan.

"Belt it down, boy. Show Toby you'da made your daddy proud."

Gogan glared over the table. He did not understand, and each betrayal cut him deeper.

But he was not yet out of patience.

He drank.

Buck sent Toby to the kitchen for a second six-pack. Another round. Then a fourth: Toby's turn, then Gogan's.

"Come on. Just put one away for Papa." It was nothing but a sneer now.

Gogan knew it would make him sick. He had barely taken a sip before he vomited.

It happened too fast for him to turn away, so he soiled his shirt and jeans. He started to stand but doubled over and threw up again, sinking back in the chair.

He felt a hand on his arm.

"Finish it."

He raised his face slowly. "Shut up."

Buck slammed his hand into Gogan's shoulder, knocking him to the floor.

"Don't you tell me to shut up, you little bastard! You bastard! I didn't ask for you! But your ma's stupid, and your old man's too dumb or too broke to buy a safe." He yanked him up and shook him. "What do you say to me? What do you say to me!"

Gogan could not stand. His uncle's face blurred. His shoulder ached.

But all he really felt was that one word.

He had forgotten Toby was there. It made no difference. Everything he could muster went into making that one phrase.

He almost smiled as the words slurred out. "Shut up, Antoine."

In spite of the sickness, the liquor, Gogan could see the surprise, the wound, and then the fury in Buck's eyes.

When the fist caught his jaw, he had already begun to fall.

Before he was fully awake, he smelled the rankness and felt the cold. He might have shivered if he had had the strength. He was lying down and realized he must be on the couch. His head was very heavy, and the side of his face was numb. Something cool moved from temple to temple. His eyelids fluttered.

"How ya doin'?" Toby said softly, without urgency, as if they were meeting in church.

Gogan started to sit. His jaw throbbed, and his head swam. He sank back.

Toby draped the washrag across Gogan's forehead and readjusted the ice pack against his cheek. "Yeah, well, you's pretty sick there." He half chuckled, "'Course, it's kinda lucky. If you and Buck hadn'ta been so skewered, he'da broke somethin' on you for sure."

"Yeah." Gogan tried to raise himself again. "Where's he at?"

"Buck? Oh, out coolin' his heels somewheres like always. He's sorry to hit you, Gogan." Toby wet the rag again in the bucket there beside them. "Says he's always hurtin' the wrong people. You gave him call, he says, but it's his fault." He shook his head. "Don't take much to that name you called him."

"You know it?" Gogan asked, surprised.

Toby stiffened. Took a breath. "Stick around here long as me," he said softly, "not much you don't know."

"Where'd you hear it?" Gogan had managed to sit up straight now.

"Oh, Bobi used to call him that sometimes."

"Bobby?"

Toby paused, uncertain. "His wife, of course," he said brusquely.

Gogan settled his hands behind his head. "So that's her name." He was not so dizzy now. "Shit." He paused a minute. "What's she like, Toby?"

He wrung out the washrag. "Oh, you know. Nice lady. Friendly . . ."

"She pretty?"

"Oh, she's pretty all right. Damn pretty."

"Uncle Buck'd only want 'em pretty, I guess." Gogan touched his jaw gingerly. "So why'd they bust up?"

Toby reached for some ice cubes floating in the bucket. "They's just not gettin' on after a while."

"They have a fight?"

"Yeah," Toby said tentatively, turning toward the kitchen. "They had lots of those."

"What about?"

"Hell, what do folks fight about?"

"What'd they fight about when she left?"

"Sweet Jesus!" Toby wheeled around. "You think I's around to ask? Buck never told . . ."

"Stick around here long as you, not much you wouldn't know, seems to me." Gogan smirked weakly, but he knew he was the catbird. "You know, or why the hell make a stink about it? I won't say nothin'," he coaxed, starting to rise.

Toby sighed, then pulled a chair over and straddled it back to front.

"All right. Now you settle on back, Gogan." His gentle hand sent Gogan back into the sofa. "You oughta know what there is to know. But you talk, and I'll bust your ass three times worse than it's already busted." He crossed his arms and leaned against his wrists, lowered his voice. "See, that last year, Buck's drinkin' more than he oughta, gettin' feisty in the bars and all, so Bobi's naggin' about it too much maybe. So this one night, he comes in all cut and says there's greasers after him and gets his gun to wait for 'em. Well, Bobi's just scared green and tells him to put that gun away, and they'll go call the sheriff. But he says he don't want no sheriff around 'cause he's gonna learn them greasers. She keeps on bellyachin', but he hears somethin' outside and lets go on it. Then she goes pretty near crazy, I hear, so he locks her up. In the closet, you know. Yanks the wardrobe over to block the door. She's in there bangin' and squallin' most of the night while he's waitin' for them greasers. He says he heard somethin' beller when he fired, but I never heard 'bout no greaser gettin' hurt that night.

"Anyhow, next morning, Buck lets Bobi out. She hightails it for the bathroom and won't come out. Won't talk to him. So he lays down for a while finally, and when he wakes up, she's washin' dishes, so he figures things is okay.

"But when he's ready to go out, he can't find the shotgun. So he says to Bobi, he says, 'Whatta you done with my gun?' And she says, real quiet, 'You got no need for a gun, Buck McMurtry.' And he says for her to tell him, and she says no, so they start fightin', and Buck, well, Buck goes a little crazy, I guess, and he started . . . starts to hurt her, and when he hurt her . . . enough, she says, 'It's down in the gully by the oak grove.' So he heads out to get it, and she says, 'Yeah, you go and get it, goddamn you, 'cause I'm gonna find me a man who don't need no gun to prove nothin' to me or nobody!'"

Toby took a deep breath. "And when he come back, she's gone."

There was a dark pause then.

Gogan leaned forward, then stood, and walked unsteadily to the open door. He leaned on the jamb and breathed deep.

"He go lookin' for her?"

"Nope," Toby said softly.

"When you see her after that?"

"Never said I seen her!"

Gogan did not turn. "Musta seen her. He never told you that story."

"Evaline seen her," Toby murmured unwilling. "'Bout two years after. Bobi's shacked up with some new guy, up in the Valley somewheres. Had a couple of kids like she always wanted. She's passin' through to see her sister in Campo. Called Evaline. Needed cash like always."

Gogan looked out into the warm spring night. "Oh," he whispered hoarsely.

It was kids.

It was a funny word for children, rock hard, and it fell through him, down into him from his ears to his gut like a plumb in a well.

He almost understood. Not entirely. Incompletely. Not in a way that could be spoken exactly. But he knew now there were other secrets, secrets darker than a soft, French name or a baby who wasn't supposed to be. Secrets to explain what made a gun and the hope of a greaser dead more precious than a woman's peace of mind. That there was something—for all his strength and courage and rage—that Buck had not been able to give his Bobi.

Kids.

All Gogan had known was a single word, a name, and he could not see until that moment what it had come to mean.

Kids.

No kids.

"So she called him Antoine."

"Sometimes." Toby's voice was a slow, sad murmur. "Maybe when she thought nobody's listenin'."

There was a weight on Gogan's chest, and the night began to soften at the edges. He choked, cleared his throat.

"You can get on now, Toby. I better turn in, I guess."

Gogan watched the truck roll away, back into the ranch, into the deeper night whose stars glimmered uncountable nearly to the horizon. He turned in the other direction, where the dull glow of a thousand streetlights reached high into the black.

He wondered where Buck was.

On the doorsill, he stopped.

It was far from dawn.

He did not go to bed when he went inside.

That night, the road was a stranger to him.

He did not know curves, and bumps came where they did not belong. The pickup tore through the black, up hillocks and rises, along gentle valley floors, down the bone-gray veins of dirt barely distinguishable from the fields beside them. There was no sound but the engine's roar and whine and the tires' muffled thud. He took a swig from the whiskey bottle from time to time, till once on a turn it jumped from his hand and spewed on his trousers and the cab floor.

He did not stop.

Sure as stone in the haze of liquor, he rushed on toward silence.

The oak grove loomed before him. Buck woke from a sleep not sleep. The truck purred forward, creaking over ruts. Still far from the trees, he stopped, took the shotgun from the rack, and got out.

The air was cool as he crept wily in spite of the whiskey, a hunter because he had to be. Whispering through the damp brush—half-afraid, half-triumphant, half-electric with expectation—he carried the gun loosely, forgotten, as if it were his own flesh.

Their voices first were but a murmur of wind. Then one rose in a shrill laugh, followed by the burble of churned water. Buck bit his hand to strangle a giggle, imagining how he might shoot: above their heads to watch them scatter or, better, into the pond, toward the other side, where the shot would ski and sting the water. Perhaps even fire at them with the barrel low, so the pellets would ricochet off the ground and buzz past them like angry wasps.

He slipped closer, picking his way gently through that barbed wire he himself had strung. The voices came clearer, high or low, sometimes louder. He could see them, too—at first like smoke, vague blurs of thicker starlight. Then they began to assume shape, running almost silent on the banks or lounging in the water—smooth, wet-glistening blue. There were half a dozen, maybe seven. He could distinguish their sex only by how they moved, for though they all floated through the velvet night, two passed with special softness over the leafed and unresonant earth.

Alone, he could watch without fear of wonder or need for ridicule. No one beside him made him leer or laugh. He stood, half in a dream for liquor and the vision, just far enough away that the language of these strangers seemed mystic, rare, and their nakedness—stuff of garish bars and hard flash photos—was magic, pure as it must have been before there was sin and cities and women who came and hurt and were hurt and then went away.

But his wonder forced him on, sliding breathless in the dark from behind one tree to the next. The voices grew harder, the words more distinct. The bodies lost their softness. The shell of a six-pack perched on a rock. Someone swore, and a girl's voice answered with the same ugly word. He picked her out, walking—her hand searching his body as his searched hers—beside a tall boy whose wet hair rose like the crest of some ridiculous bird.

Buck tensed, and he felt the forgotten gun in his hands.

He moved toward the final tree before the bank.

"Hey!"

He leapt back.

"Hey! Who's there?"

"What?"

"I saw somebody. In the trees. There."

"Oh, probably just some redneck out to get his rocks off."

They all laughed.

"Hey! Come on out! Nothin' but us plain neked folks out here."

They laughed again. All together.

He stepped slowly from behind the tree, gun raised.

The laughter died.

Buck walked forward through the starlight, toward the group of them who now made a tight V, the tall boy at the apex. Naked, all of them. He almost, by reflex, averted his eyes. But he did not. He drew closer, the gun leveled.

The ones at the rear began to back away.

He could see them clearly now. Five boys. Two girls.

And it was not right. It was not right that they were here naked. He had learned that long ago, there in Oklahoma in a hillbilly church with a hillbilly preacher who could talk about sin and shame and Hell.

And it was not right that they would be here still. Even when the ranch was gone, when the power lines were up. And the houses. When the trailer had been pulled back deep, deeper into the spread, shrinking ever smaller.

When he could no longer walk here.

He was always losing. And them, always winning. The fast talkers, the city slickers, the smart-ass sailors, the faggot land boys. And those hard, mean women, those Mrs. Merritts, those . . .

He stopped. "What in hell you doin' 'round here, boy?"

"Taking a dip, man. You can understand that."

Buck could make out the cool eyes, some light color, in the half-dark.

"This here's private property. You figure you can come up here any-time and run around bare-ass just 'cause you come to feel like it?"

"Nobody seemed to mind." The words came slowly. "You a cop?"

"Jerry, don't make trouble." The girl was breathless, urgent.

The boy pushed her gently away.

Buck glanced at her briefly, contemptuously.

"Yeah. I'm a deputy."

"Got a badge?"

Buck's eyes narrowed. He clenched the stock a little tighter. "In my truck."

"Ought to carry it with you."

Buck laid his finger heavier on the trigger.

"Seems like you shouldn't smart-ass me, boy. I just might blow off them little ballsa yours."

"Bad idea." The words were steady as before. "All these people around. They'd stick you away for a good long time."

That surety. That vicious, goddamn surety of hippies and sailors and city people: jibing, pushing, stinging like leather. Winning. They were always winning! Buck jammed the butt into his body as if to make good his threat.

"Goddamn it!"

But he did not mean to fire, simply frighten, only silence that cocksure, smart-mouth bastard from the city. But then, from the corner of his eye, he saw her, stumbling forward as if pushed, face contorted perhaps in tears, crying: "No! Please, no! You don't need the gun, you don't need . . ."

He swiveled and struck clumsily the trigger, and there was an explosion, then another—the first sharp, the second like a sack of old clothes falling as she flew apart before him and the fine spray of her dying wet his face.

Then he was running, running oblivious to the wails and shrieks, dodging the trees that loomed and grasped around him. Away. Running away to the truck to escape the smell of blood. The screams. His legs pumped, and the gun bounced loose and worthless at his side.

The pickup appeared. He jumped into the cab, mechanically releasing the brake and grinding gears. Then he was gone in a cloud of starstruck dust.

In that familiar closeness, with the groan of the engine and the reek of whiskey, he might have hoped for solace, but there was none. His feet played the pedals. He fingered the wheel and fiddled the shift. He maneuvered the curves and bumps. But there before him, more clearly, he saw the unseen, what it is impossible to see, over and over: *She crying words he did not hear and he turned and fired, and the shells burst from the barrel in a spew of death that tore her to pieces before the sound had died and her blood. . . . He took a step forward and caught the motion and saw her naked body, arms extended, and her little girl face twisted, and she said something about the gun, and his finger twitched*—bang!—*steel spittle like a dirty kiss blowing her into leaves and the earth and the rain of blood and . . . He took a step forward, man-to-man, and the woman rushed to stop him like she always did saying, "You got no need . . ." and he had to hurt her, Bobi, for shaming him, not meaning to—or did she?—in the night, and now she wanted the gun, and he turned, and the breasts that would know no child of his, no son of a girl-named father, disappeared as if detonated from within and her blood. . . . She lunged toward him with the knife, and the others circled round, all city-smart, all loose-mouthed, naked winners laughing. "Now we'll fix him, fix him, finally now forever . . ." And he fired the gun!*

The truck skied into a turn, and the right wheels jumped the lip of the ditch. It teetered for a moment, skidding forward, then he was thrown across the seat as the pickup slammed on its side.

Buck—crumpled, momentarily stunned—began to stir, the shotgun curled in the tangle of his body. He unwound himself wearily, till fear of fire waked him and he was suddenly kicking a shower of glass to escape into the night.

He started to run, took a dozen steps, and vomited. Then again. His head spun. His vision telescoped to pinpoints as he fell toward a faint. Bracing himself with the barrel, he staggered a few more paces, gasping. He raised his head and saw, in the distance, the light from the trailer.

Doggedly, painfully, he began to trot toward home.

o o o

Gogan, on the couch, shuddered suddenly, utterly awake.

He pulled on a shirt and stepped outside.

The night had not changed. The sky blossomed with stars, and, as Gogan's eyes adjusted to the dark, the familiar shapes of the yard emerged: the propane tanks, the incinerator, the toolshed. The glow of the city still stained one horizon. Dawn seemed no closer than before.

There had been a noise.

He stepped toward the edge of the grade. He heard running, someone slipping on the gravel of the drive.

"Uncle Buck?"

No answer.

"Uncle Buck!"

He scooped up a splintered fence post.

"Uncle Buck!" He could hear panting. "Hey!"

He leapt forward, the post cocked, and landed nearly face-to-face with his uncle.

Gogan smiled, relieved. "Well, what the hell . . ."

Then he looked harder and saw Buck, like a broken kite, the gun dangling from his hand. Gogan took his arm and slung it over his shoulder.

"Come on."

He set his uncle on the couch, brought a glass of water.

When he raised Buck's face to make him drink, he saw the blood. "You're hurt."

He ran his fingers along Buck's scalp, looking for the wound.

"What're you doin'?" Buck shouted, grabbing Gogan's wrist. "What the hell you doin'?"

The boy yanked free, angry. "Goddamn it! You're hurt somewheres. What'd you do? Wreck the truck? Half the county musta heard! Out drunk . . . !" He caught himself, sighed, lowered his voice. "Sit down. You got blood all over you."

"Ain't my blood."

Gogan faltered.

"Ain't my blood."

Gogan shook his head. "Boy, you musta really banged yourself on the dash. Just simmer down. . . ." He reached out.

Buck grabbed his extended hand. "Where's my gun?"

"What?"

"My gun. What'd you do with my gun!"

He twisted Gogan's arm.

"There! There, by the door! There."

Buck shoved the boy away and gathered up the weapon in one clumsy motion, then dove for the closet. "Where's the goddamn shells!"

Hangers and clothes and shoes clattered out. He emerged with the cardboard box and opened the gun with such force that he might have broken it in half.

"They'll be comin.' Comin' any second . . ."

"Who? Who'll be comin'?" Gogan followed at Buck's heels. "What happened? Sit down. We gotta find out what you did to your head."

Buck spun around, whispering hoarsely, deliberately: "Ain't my blood!"

Gogan knew then.

"Oh God, you killed somebody. . . ."

It was as if Buck heard the words for the first time, had not thought them himself. He spread his arms.

"I had to, Gogan. They's gonna fix me. All of 'em down there around me at the pond and she says, 'Now we'll fix him!' and she's got a knife. . . ."

"A girl. Oh, Jesus, Jesus. You killed a girl. . . ." Gogan sat down, rocking his head in his hands.

"I had to, Gogan. They'da fixed me, Gogan. You gotta see." Buck slumped beside his nephew, kneading the boy's shoulder, the shoulder that still ached. "I had to, doncha see? They'da fixed me. I had to."

Gogan wished he believed it. He wanted to believe it more than anything he had ever believed. But nobody faced a shotgun with only a knife and threatened what no man could allow.

But Buck believed it. Gogan could tell.

The lie became true in the telling.

And then he was afraid. There would be more blood. There would have to be.

He tried to ask for the shotgun. No words came out. Bobi had tried. She had tried years before, that woman Buck loved hopelessly even as he loathed her. No sister's big-city bastard would take it from him now.

Faintly, Gogan heard sirens beyond the next rise, passing the oak grove. Buck stirred beside him, tensing in fear and courage, raw as a hillbilly.

There was no chance left for talking.

"The pistol in the nightstand?"

Buck, by the door, gun raised, spoke softly. "What?"

"You're gonna need some help."

Gogan heard a sigh that was almost a laugh.

"In the drawer by the bed."

He crept through the black, pawed past the aspirin bottle and pack of Kleenex and old pens and Vicks, then returned, crouching there behind his uncle, the gun butt cold in his hand.

The sirens had died, but a new sound rose—tires in the gravel and engines louder for the stillness. Red lights, redder than the blood on Buck's face, whirled through the perfect night.

Gogan's finger toyed with the trigger.

The city was coming. Paved streets. Boxwood hedges. Laundromats, gas stations, streetlights, and stop signs. And people, thousands to raise thousands more: accountants and builders and hippies and punks, sailors and salesmen, whores and queers, movers and makers of a world that had no place for a man named Antoine.

Gogan wondered if it would have a place for him.

"Gogan."

"Yeah."

"Gogan, I'm sorry for what happened."

He could see him, though there was no light: every muscle, every scar—the lined and bloodied face.

The accumulated wounds of a man out of time.

"I'm sorry, too."

The cars abruptly halted on the drive.

Gogan raised his gun through the darkness.

Reprise

for Kate

Esther wasn't pretty, never had been. She was thin and freckled and, even if grownup longer than she cared to remember, still a little knock-kneed. But, as she walked into the hotel lounge that evening, it was certain, too, that she wasn't homely. She had a shy, troubled walk and a sober, intelligent face that lent her an odd girlishness, made her undeniably attractive for her very vulnerability, like some plain but treasured object from an era when life was simpler.

She glanced around the badly lit bar but did not find who she was looking for. She felt vaguely embarrassed and stood a little too long in the doorway, which embarrassed her more, before sidling quickly through the tables to a booth in the corner.

"And what can I get you tonight?"

The waitress had that easy, almost unnatural beauty Esther always associated with California, the beauty that comes from being young and pretty in the first place, then from simply walking in that unreal light of beaches where skin turns browner and hair turns blonder and limbs grow longer, more supple.

All it had done this week for Esther was make her freckles darker. "Just coffee."

"Coffee?"

"Yes." It was too sharp. She tried to laugh. "I'm the designated driver."

The waitress went away.

She took out a cigarette. She had not smoked in years. But at this exhibition, distinct from all the others, she had started again for some reason.

She paused for an instant as she lit up and smiled.

They had both smoked in France. He smoked much too much, and she perhaps took up the habit to make him feel less guilty. At night, after Samantha was finally asleep, they would sit on opposite ends of the windowsill, there in the two a.m. darkness, naked, smoking Gitanes. They had only one window. But the light was good, he always insisted. The light was the best you could ask for.

The coffee came, steaming, in a cup like a parfait glass. She drank it in small, distracted sips. Ever since Paris, she had never liked American coffee.

They were silly to go to Paris. It would have made more sense to go to New York, come here to Los Angeles, or—if it had to be Europe— Greece or Sardinia, southern Spain or someplace in Portugal. But they were set on Paris, because they had both read too many memoirs and novels, old manifestos and art history books, and, at twenty-two and twenty-four, could still determinedly fool themselves that the city could not have changed so much in fifty years. For the six months before they left, he had worked two jobs, skipped lunch, stopped painting, while she stayed at home with the baby: guilty not to be working, guilty to be drawing, guilty for the child who wasn't even his. To salve her conscience, she collected bottles in the neighborhood, hoarded newspapers, clipped coupons. She entered every contest, milked every special offer. Her only pleasures all day were Samantha sucking at her breast, cooing in the crib, bouncing in the backpack baby carrier. He got home at nine-thirty, by Friday almost walleyed. They would eat soup and talk about his day in the plant and evening at the bookstore, her latest coup at the grocer's, and how Samantha was growing and growing.

And how it would be in Paris, of course.

She looked at her watch. The coffee dregs were cold in the bottom of the cup. He might have decided not to come at all. It was she who had dropped him a note when she saw his name on the list of exhibitors. He didn't seem surprised to hear from her despite all the years. It was he who suggested they have a drink.

He had always been a drinker, too much of one. He was a friend of Rafe's, and she had first met him when he staggered by one evening to help Rafe kill a bottle of Old Crow. He had begun coming more and more often: the three of them on the living room floor, the whiskey or cheap wine making the rounds, weaving through the conversation till it was gone. Then she got pregnant, and Rafe went away. He went to Alaska to work on the pipeline, to provide for the baby, he said. He wrote at first, then only sent money. By the time Samantha was born, Esther hadn't heard from him in months. Tim had moved in by then.

She saw him coming across the lounge, that familiar loping walk. Even in the almost darkness, she was struck by how young he looked, younger even than he had looked the last time she had seen him. A smile on that irreproachably open Greek face, he came quickly, but it was as if she watched him in slow motion, as if all her senses were heightened to take advantage of each split second of his arriving. His mouth still fell in that quizzical, comic grin, and those thick, brown curls broke over his collar just as before.

He was huskier than he had been in Paris.

She realized she was breathing faster.

"Esther! Esther, my love." He reached around the table to hug her, pecked her on the cheek. "Why did we wait so long?"

She returned his warmth, sincere if a little distant, squeezing his shoulders, harder than she remembered them, brushing her lips over that stubble he could never control. He even had the same smell: earth and sweat and the astringency of paint.

They sat down. He asked the waitress for a scotch. For a moment, they just smiled across the table, innocent and pleased.

"You haven't changed." She shook her head. "It's silly to say so, but you haven't."

"Oh, come on. . . ."

"No, it's true."

It was true, and she was aware suddenly that it discomfited her. It was not quite right that he should look so young, so utterly unspoiled after all the years, and, in that instant, she realized it was not natural, that, unlike before, his youth was synthetic, the calculated result of taking care of himself.

"But what are you doing now?" he asked. "Where is it? Santa Fe?"

"That's right." She smiled. "I've got a little gallery there. I put on insubstantial little exhibits of what I do or what I like. The only rule is no Georgia O'Keefe imitations and no Navajo motifs."

He laughed.

"What about you? Your name turns up in the journals sometimes."

He sighed. "Oh, I sold out." He raised his hand to stay her objection. "I was never really good enough to avoid it. But it's all right. I've got a house in Hermosa and do shows on Melrose and down in New-port. I did the lobby of the Intercontinental in Maui last year—tropi-cal murals, phony Gauguin." He smirked. "Just the kind of thing we always loathed."

She smiled faintly, unsure how seriously he meant it.

"And have you . . ." His drink came. "Have you, ah . . ." He wiggled his ring finger.

"Gotten married?"

"That's it."

"No." She took out another cigarette. "Want one?"

He shook his head. "Gave 'em up years ago."

"You!"

"Yep." He played with the swizzle stick. "Can't smoke and pump iron."

They were silent just seconds too long, long enough for both of them to know the question that would have to come next. Her hand shook, just slightly, as she struck the match. She slumped back and blew the first drag out long, to relax.

"So, you haven't either."

"Haven't?"

She snuffed a nervous laugh. "Gotten married."

"Oh, no." He tried too hard to be light about it. "No, even in any-thing-goes California, we haven't progressed that far. But I have been a pretty faithful fellow the last couple years."

"What's his name?"

"Kerry."

She was pleased at how easy it was for her. "Does he paint, too?"

Tim laughed. "Oh, God no. God, I couldn't live with another painter." He cleared his throat, twisting that funny face in half-shamed apology. "You know what I mean. He's an electrician. Twenty-five.

From Colorado. He's no great shakes for conversation, but he's terrific for a tumble."

She flinched. That was his word for it. The one he had used their very first time, the night he came by after they hadn't seen each other in ages. Her fifth month. Six weeks since the last fifty dollars with no return address had arrived from Alaska.

They each had a beer.

She began to cry. "Oh, Tim, he won't come back. He won't! And what'll I do with a baby? Oh, God, Tim, what'll I do?"

And finally, as he held her, when she had quieted, he said: "I think what you need is a tumble"—he hunched down to kiss her—"with me."

"Well, that's for the best, I suppose," she said quickly, too brightly. She took a long pull on her cigarette but couldn't keep it from coming out: "That was the Frenchman's long suit, too, wasn't it?"

"Which one?"

This time she stifled the flinch. "You know. The first one. What was his name?"

Tim furrowed his brow in a parody of remembering. "René? Marcel?"

His name was Alain, of course. She could never forget that. She knew Tim hadn't either.

She glanced at her watch. "Are you going to the reception at seven?"

"Lord no. Those things are always dreary."

He was right. They were dreary. She hadn't planned to go. But now she wanted to.

"I really have to. Friends. Tamara would never speak to me if I didn't show."

He killed his drink. "Is it downstairs?"

"On the arcade."

"I'll walk you."

They did not speak on the stairs, or almost the entire way down the promenade, past the swimsuit boutique, the knickknack shop, the jewelry store. Finally, they could hear the hum from the opening.

"How's Sammy?"

It came suddenly, almost plaintively, and it struck her harder than it should have for that.

"She's fine," Esther said casually, smiling. "Growing so fast. She doesn't look a bit like me, thank God."

"Oh, Esther."

"Or a bit like Rafe," she added, "which is even better."

They had come to the door.

"And does she still think I'm her daddy?"

The fake blitheness of it scalded her. Esther turned on him angrily, all the pain of that second abandonment—in a foreign place with no warning at all, for reasons so incontestable that it hurt to understand—welling up from wherever it had been buried for so long.

But when his eyes caught hers, the anger went away. In the glare of the gallery lights, she could see the crows' feet the isometrics couldn't hide completely, a few stray strands of gray in his hair.

"No," she said. "No, I told her her daddy went away before she was born." That was true. "But I told her that when she was very little, when she first learned to talk, there was another man who was her daddy for a while." That was a lie. "Who loved her very much."

He nodded, smiled mechanically. "Well, that's good."

"Esther. Esther!"

He took a long step back. "I think you're being paged. Are you in L.A. long?"

"A couple more days."

"We should have dinner or something."

"Well, I'm pretty busy, but . . ."

"Esther!"

She sighed. "Just a second." She crossed the threshold into the gallery. "In a minute, Tam. Hi! I'll be there in a minute."

When she turned back, he was disappearing down the arcade.

He was running.

Fellatio

for another Harry

"Fellatio—that's cocksucking—," he explained, "has only achieved popularity in recent years, when men habitually began to bathe. Before, our only choice was the unspeakable crime against nature."

I could feel him smiling against my chest.

"Happily, we live in an age of redoubled possibilities."

It was ten days past his eighteenth birthday, but the first he had been free. When I saw him as I came off my shift at the mill, I felt a stab in my heart. Both for what would happen now and for what would happen later. It was a dithery helplessness—something a man should never feel. But Harry could make me into a girl that way, even if I always played the man.

"The unspeakable crime does have its points, don't you think?" He slithered his body next to mine. He was the snake in the Garden, as I had often told him. His tongue was in my ear. "Am I still your sissy now, my Paddy-Cake?"

And I, knowing what had to come, could only breathe, "You are always my sissy boy, Harry."

I am not a man who talks much. I am not a man who feels free. I am not a man who understands the world. I grew up in the fields, and that is not a happy place to be. Do not let people fool you. They speak of those lovely times in the country, but the country is hard and coarse and mean. It is dust and mud and drear. The country means a body sore from labor, day to week to year. It is bruises and cuts and broken bones, infection and tetanus and gangrene. It is a heedless sun and a mist that chills the marrow. It is work like work has been for centuries, with nothing changing.

Times were hard, and so I had to leave. I was the second brother, after all. I crossed the sea. Not to America. To England.

Perhaps I was lucky.

I am a good worker. A good husband. A good provider.

I am the father of five daughters, and I go to Mass.

Though not every week.

I was only a boy when I came, and I met Alice not much after. In the year or so before, you would think I had many adventures, but you would be wrong. I had little money. I had even less confidence. Harry said I must have been pretty then.

Pretty.

That is what he said.

But there, alone and Irish, I did not feel pretty, even among the other Irish who were angry and sad and away from home and would cheat a countryman as quick as piss in the morning.

That very first time, Harry said I was robust.

And then he giggled.

I had never known a man to giggle.

My Alice had red hair, and I with my black hair loved redheads, and so we were married, and she would not mind me saying we had a fine time, the two of us, even after the first girls were born. Maybe we kept at it because we always wanted a boy.

It is only now I thank God there were none.

But Harry had the softest skin. Softer than Alice's. It was some magic, silken thing, that skin. I felt rude and dirty against it, my rough hands and the stubble on my chin. But he always told me that it was those things about me that he loved.

Oh, he was foolish—that Harry!—in the way only the rich can be. In Ireland, I did not know rich boys. When would a boy like me have had the chance? Perhaps he was just careless. I mean that the way it sounds, which is something Harry taught me—to think of what words say. Rich people, especially children of rich people, think they have no cares. So they are care-*less*. And it was certain when I met him that Harry seemed somebody so different from me and everyone I had ever known that I could not parse him. There in the underpass, the trains pounding overhead as my shift let out. I was late that night, having stayed to warn the next ones that the third loom could not be counted on. It was twilight, close to dark.

And he stopped me in the gloom and said, "Hello there."

He stepped in front of me. Harry was shameless. He wore a fine suit of blue wool and carried a cane, which looked very silly. He was so young. He had the fresh, soft face of a child, like I might once have had back in Ireland, long ago.

But much younger then than he was now.

"Hullo."

I was surly. What was I to say? When you come from peasants, you learn the language of peasants—abrupt and grudging. I had worked very hard and was very tired, and a sixteen-year-old boy in a suit that cost more than I made in a month planted himself before me. What for the love of Mary could he want of me?

He looked at me, smiled—and his smile was beautiful, those teeth so straight and white—and he said, "I like you."

That seemed a strange thing to say, for what about me was there for him to like? I was forty then. My face was lined and my body square, and my legs were squat, and my hair was thin and going to gray. I was not an interesting person. I worked in the mill. I had five daughters, and I was Irish and Catholic and did not really belong here.

But I stopped. And I said, "And why should that be?"

I might have said so many other things. But there was something in that smile, something in that suit, something in a silly, snobbish youngster who had stopped me and not made me draw my knife because he planned to rob me, but who had said, with no explanation at all, that he liked me.

"Do we need a reason?"

He smiled again.

It was only then I saw him—not his clothes, not his posture. Who he was.

I am not stupid. He was rich, he was young, he was under a bridge at seven-thirty at night. It was 1913. And he himself was sixteen. I had been in England long enough. I had lived in town long enough. I had heard the stories in the mill from time to time of extra money to be had.

I knew what he probably wanted.

Back home, when I was twelve, my cousin Laurence came to visit. Walking, it had taken him two days. He seemed some kind of hero to me. When he told my parents what was happening in Queenstown, which was someplace so magically different from any place I had ever known, I simply listened with a wide-eyed wonder. When it was time for bed, he shared mine, and, in the middle of the night, he did things to me. He said he did it with his brothers Thomas and Patrick and Michael and William.

I never thought anything about it really.

We went to a rooming house. He paid. He did to me what Laurence had made me do to him. Unlike then, I felt I was the one who acted. But really it was just the same. Laurence had done what he wanted to do. Harry did what he wanted to do. And I? I was simply the conduit, the channel through which desire flowed and so was set free.

A week later, he was there again.

We went to the rooming house. He had a lovely way of taking off my clothes. By then, with Alice and me — the both of us were always so tired, especially as we got older—after getting the girls to bed, it was fast, and we did it because we ought to as good Catholics. But we did not have, as we once did, the kind of hugging and snuggling before and after, for who has the time when work presses on your shoulders five days a week and a half on Saturday, when there is money to be made if you work even more, so the children can have sweets and shoes and, now and then, a new dress to sport on the street, beneath the gaze of other fathers who know that, in the end, you can provide?

So, to feel my shoes, my shirt, my trousers not coming off but somehow vanishing . . . Harry was a magician, a hypnotist. He must have mesmerized me, so I could not resist nor comprehend what he was doing. How had he made me naked? And he naked, too? As if he had clapped his hands and his clothes fell away. Then his hands, his fingers, rode over my body like a breeze, like something I remembered from age six or seven, the feel of the slightest wind off the sea on a warm summer day. I do admit, I wondered where he learned that—

how to make a workingman's merest clay into ether beneath his touch. I often thought him wicked, especially after we were done and I was walking to the tram, to my Alice. I thought him wicked and evil and the spawn of the devil.

And yet, I had known no such pleasure in all my days. Without cease. Without pause. Of all that Harry gave me, that was the greatest gift. In that hour, week to week, I there stout and broken, Irish in a land that had no use for me but labor, Harry would take all the pains I had acquired (the strains and sprains and arthritis and lumbago) and he would, for the littlest while, ease them, soothe them, blot them away. He would make me again that boy who had arrived with a sack of all his worldly goods in Liverpool, now on his own, now to make a life.

o o o

We were naked in bed, my freckled sweetheart in my arms, half-sleeping. For two years now, he had let me do whatever I chose. But, of course, that is not true, for it was what he wanted. But he had made my wants his and his wants mine, set my own tired body free to find out exactly what bodies were for. He was different from my Alice, my own.

Had they known on the factory floor!

But then, perhaps more than I knew, each had our Harry.

"I'm going to France," he said softly.

It was a stone in my gut, a fist to my face. I grabbed him without thinking. I had never hugged him like that. He was the one who hugged me.

"Harry! Don't, Harry."

I knew. I knew from the mill. I knew what was happening. Harry read the papers. Harry's parents read the papers. Harry's aunts and uncles and friends read the papers.

They believed them because they wanted to believe them. They were rich people, so they had to believe despite shattered sons and husbands and cousins and nephews and friends.

But I knew.

Again, I felt like a girl. I felt like I was telling him not to be a brave man. Not to be a man at all. But I knew what was happening. To thousands. To millions. Not just Irish boys, though those were the boys I cared about most. But Welshmen and Scots and English boys, too. Australians and Canadians. Frenchmen and Germans. Austrians and Italians and Turks and Belgians.

There in the mill, we heard and we saw—the bodies coming back, how they came back if they came back at all. And we saw the ones who did not die but went mad instead, and the ones again in our midst with no legs, no arms, no eyes, no face. I had been to the services. Been to the wakes.

"Don't go, Harry." I paused for a second. I do not believe I said it. "For me."

He looked at me, my redheaded boy, with a funny astonishment. "But I have to go, dearest. Everyone is going."

My heart twisted because I realized then that he was indeed a boy, one like I had been when I had landed in England, so sure of my promise. And then I thought of Ireland. How everyone is going. How, from the time I was born, all I ever heard about was leaving.

But all those places somehow meant work or freedom or, at the least, food in your belly.

But Harry was headed toward the dark.

It was very hard for me then—me with my Alice, with my five daughters—but, in that moment, I knew what was to come. I knew exactly who was rich and who was poor, who was young and who was old, who would leave with a giggle and a spring in his step and who would remember this moment forever.

We were together three times more, and the last time he was in uniform. The landlady remarked on how fine he looked. That last time, I did things I had never done and I would never admit I did them today. I can see his face, the look of someone who cannot understand what is happening but, whatever it is, he will take it and take again, and my Irish heart aches.

o o o

They brought him back barely two months later.

I stood outside the church. The man who would talk to me after the funeral—a young officer not unlike Harry who somehow understood what had happened between Harry and me—said he was on the barbed wire for seven hours.

For much of that, he was not dead.

But with the machine guns, they could do nothing.

There was nothing anyone could do.

All these years later, I think of him: naked and fair, sprawled on that rooming house bed, inviting me, teasing me, telling me—who never thought a thing about himself—that I am manly and handsome and worthy. Alice, of course, in her way, has told me the same. But it was Harry—all his richness and his naughty mouth and his endless ideas of what we could do—that I remember, and that brings him before me, under a railroad bridge: fresh as an apple, green as an emerald, sure as a prophet.

My Harry.

My own.